A Vote For Love

JEA HAWKINS

Wicked Hearts Publishing

PUBLISHED BY WICKED HEARTS PUBLISHING

COPYRIGHT 2017 BY JEA HAWKINS

COVER ART BY SATYR DESIGNS

FIRST EDITION
ISBN-13: 978-1547181490

Chapter 1

ONE KISS. ONE SCORCHING, passionate kiss from the most beautiful woman she had ever seen in her life, and then she was lost. Everything was an orgasmic blur after that, each and every sensation still fresh in her mind. The woman in the sparkling evening gown on her knees in front of her. A searching tongue giving Hayley explosive pleasure, while Hayley's fingers clutched at the woman's perfect golden blonde hair, undoing a coif it had probably taken an hour to get right in the first place.

Hayley had never done anything like that before in her life and she doubted it would ever happen to her again. She didn't give into spontaneous, casual sex. Hell, she didn't even give into planned sex. There was no time in her life for a girlfriend, which was probably why she had unwound like a coiled spring at the very first touch.

Control, control, control. She had to regain it.

As she strode out of the supply closet moments later, she smoothed any flyaway wisps of brown hair back from her face and tightened her ponytail. Would anyone notice she had been gone so long from her station or if anything was out of place? A hasty check of her button-down white shirt, black vest, and black skirt showed her that everything was where it belonged.

Except for her panties.

She hesitated, the urge to spin on her heel and walk back the way she'd come strong. Almost overwhelming. But no. Clenching her fists, she took another second to master her emotions and then continued on her way. She had already been kept away too long. Besides, what would she say to the woman if she encountered her again? It would be too awkward. Best to get back to her post and go on as if nothing had happened.

At least it wasn't like she had to pretend to maintain her self-control. It was the one thing she was good at once she regained it. Well, that and serving people.

Since there was no retrieving the missing underwear now, she made her way around the crowd, walking at the fringes of the ballroom like a good waitress should. In her line of work, remaining unobtrusive was an important skill. No one at a fancy gala wanted to know you existed unless it was to hand them a crudité or take their empty glass. Even a "Thank you" was too much for some people when they were busy talking to other people. People who weren't waitresses. People who mattered.

When Hayley finally got back to her station at the party, her co-worker threw her a strange look. "Where are the cucumber slices?" she asked.

"What?" Hayley blinked at Kristen. Her mind was still racing, still bombarding her with images of that sensual meeting in the storage room. She compressed her lips and tried to regulate her breathing with one, long inhale.

"Don't you remember? You said you had to go to the restroom and I told you we needed additional cucumber for the water, so you said you'd get the slices from the kitchen on your way back. So where are they?"

Hayley replayed the last fifteen minutes in her head. They were the most amazing fifteen minutes of her life.

And they were also nothing to write home about, because she wouldn't dare tell anyone she had slipped into the supply closet at the back of the hotel to check her email on her phone, only to end up leaning back against the wall with one of the elegant partygoers under her skirt, giving her the greatest pleasure she'd ever experienced.

No, she wasn't about to tell anyone how she'd spread her legs so that gorgeous blonde could get up between them and work magic on Hayley with her tongue. It just wasn't the kind of thing that came up in conversation. What could she say, though?

Fortunately, Kristen saved her from speaking at all. "You were checking your email again, weren't you? Jeez, Hayley." Kristen rolled her eyes and shook her head. "Look, I know you really want that interview, but odds are it's never going to happen. You know they're going to pick some guy with money, probably someone graduating from an Ivy League school whose family can grease the palm of the right person there to make it happen. And checking your phone every five minutes isn't going to make it happen, especially on a weekend night."

The last thing Hayley had on her mind now was the fact that she needed to get job interviews or the fact that she was probably one of the poorest students attending her school. Unlike many of her peers, she didn't intend to go on to grad school, because she had to work to earn the money if she wanted to study for anything higher than a bachelor's degree. As it was, she was grateful for the full ride scholarship she'd received after passing both the ACT and SAT exams with perfect scores when she was only thirteen.

The problem with trying to earn money for her future, whether it was for even more education or just to have a place to live after college, was the only jobs available to her. The only ones with flexible hours were also low-paying, like her steady one as a barista and then the occasional waitressing gig with a friend of hers who ran a catering business. And even if he didn't have a job for her, he usually knew a place in need of a waitress for the night, like the hotel.

She tried to treat these waitressing jobs as an opportunity to learn how to network, the way the Washington D.C. bigwigs did. She studied them at these parties, listened in on their conversations, and tried to emulate some of their mannerisms. She then used that kind of savvy to get the right internships in hopes of also getting her foot in the door at a newspaper.

But it didn't work – none of the papers where she'd interned were offering jobs at the moment unless she wanted to work in a mail room. So now she had to line up her own interviews to find work after graduation. At least Kristen had given her an easy out in response to the question of where she'd been. She took it.

"Look, if I don't get that interview, I'll try for another one. It's not that big a deal. Doesn't mean I can't help but wonder if I will get it, though," Hayley said defensively. Her heart was racing as she said it, partly because she was still distracted by the lingering sensation a wetness and an unwelcome breeze between her thighs and partly because the conversation brought her mind back to what really mattered. Jump-starting her career by getting the job of her dreams, so she could continue on the path she'd planned for her life.

Of course it was a big deal or she wouldn't be checking her phone every five minutes. Using personal cell phones was strictly forbidden on the job, though, especially one like this where she was working a gala filled with wealthy people who expected the wait staff to jump at their every whim. But her phone had buzzed with an email notification a half-hour ago and even though it was eight o'clock at night, she couldn't help but check it.

They still had another two hours at the party, which also meant another two hours to dwell on what had happened in that supply closet. She had to find a way to shift her mindset because now it was an awful muddle.

"Fine. I'll get the cucumber." Kristen gave her one last glare of disapproval. As soon as she left, Hayley let out a sigh of relief.

It wasn't that Kristen was unsupportive; it's just that she was very strict and by-the-book. When they were on a job, Kristen gave it her complete attention. She didn't deviate from the path set for them by the boss. That was why she would make a great prosecutor, while Hayley went on a more nebulous path as a journalist.

She looked at the plates arranged on their table and then checked the water. Both dispensers were full of water, which meant they needed more fresh cucumber slices to flavor it. How could she have forgotten?

It was easy to forget when the woman who'd been

stopping by the table all night apparently followed her to the back room, eager to share a kiss, and then…

Hayley tried to shake the thoughts from her head. She wasn't one for easy sex, but she knew the woman. Sort of. The stunning blonde was a regular at the coffee shop and they had been encountering each other for the last couple of years.

At first, Hayley had simply seen her as any other customer in the shop. Tall, polished-looking in her stylish suit, blonde hair in a perfect bun, and giving the same order every day. During the early morning rush, Hayley didn't really connect with any of the customers. On those days, she'd been up since five in the morning. Her eyes were still pretty bleary and the promise of a cup of coffee brought one customer after another. But somehow Hayley always managed to notice *her*.

Then, one weekend day, Hayley was there during lunch time after she'd had a chance to sleep in just a bit, and the woman came in the shop again. It took Hayley a moment, but it wasn't difficult to place that beautiful face. The difference was the woman wore a white button-down shirt with a blue sweater draped over her shoulders. She looked wholesome and casual, less intimidating than she did in a business suit. So Hayley struck up a brief conversation with her as she put in the order.

Something about her intrigued Hayley from that day on, though she wasn't sure what it was. Maybe it was just the way she looked or maybe it was because Hayley had seen two different sides of her. Granted, everything was based on a shallow judgment about her appearance and superficial small talk, but still…

"Fine then, space cadet. If you won't answer me, take this." Kristen had returned and slid a plate of fresh sliced cucumbers to her. "Will you fill that dispenser, while I get this one?"

Hayley nodded and did it slowly, still mulling over her thoughts.

When she thought of her coffee shop customer, she'd never gone so far as to develop a crush on her. In fact, concentrating on school had pretty much obliterated her interest in dating, romance, or even a fling. She felt like she was under pressure around the clock and that wasn't at all conducive to getting in the mood for love. Studying was her first priority. Studying and getting on the right path with her intended career.

Maybe that was her problem, though. Maybe she'd just taken every feeling she'd been suppressing since she was thirteen, dreaming of going to college, and let it all out tonight when that woman kissed her. It was a deep, lingering kiss, and then the way the woman had looked into her eyes told her there was something there. But what?

Before Hayley could question it, that gorgeous, elegant woman was between her legs, removing her panties and tasting her. Hayley briefly wondered if the woman had a similar life – rushing from work to other commitments all day, so caught up in what she had to do to succeed, that she was rarely in the mood for anything resembling love. Maybe their anonymous hook-up was a symptom of two too-busy lives, nothing more.

It certainly wasn't like Hayley had time for a girlfriend. Even in high school, she had focused on her schoolwork and after-school jobs. Not that she'd had much to pick from in her small Midwestern town anyway. Finding another gay high school student wasn't easy in rural Nebraska. Of course, the reason she'd moved to Washington D.C. wasn't to get lucky – it was to ensure she had a degree from an amazing school and her foot in the door at the newspaper of her dreams.

She had every intention of scoring a job at the Washington Post. Pushing herself hard to achieve her ambition was worth it, even if that meant she hadn't had a girlfriend since she was sixteen.

Hayley looked up and there she was by the table, that beautiful woman who had followed her into the supply closet, delivered a searing kiss and then, through some sort of unspoken acknowledgment between them, gone down on her. She was still the most gorgeous woman Hayley had ever seen – statuesque with blonde hair, green eyes, and radiating confidence. The black evening gown clung to her body, hugging every curve. The woman turned and their eyes met. For a moment, time stood still. The music faded and there were only two people in the world – Hayley and her unexpected lover.

"Are you all right?" Kristen jiggled her shoulder a bit, bringing Hayley back to the present. "You look a little dopey."

"I'm fine. Just tired. It's been a long day." Hayley dropped her gaze to the table. It was true. She was beyond exhausted. Senior year was the most difficult, but she refused to stop for even a moment. Stopping was admitting defeat and then someone – probably one of those rich, entitled guys in her classes – would get ahead, while she ate their dust.

Kristen looked sympathetic. "It's hard and I'm tired all the time, too. Can you imagine what law school is going to be like? At least you aren't going to grad school. You just get to sit down and write news and call it good."

No, she wasn't going to grad school, but journalism also wasn't as easy as Kristen made it sound. Hayley had to fight for a job at the media outlet she'd dreamed of working for since she was thirteen years old. She could always do grad school part time once she was settled, but first she needed to prove herself as a journalist. And that took time and energy, a willingness to dig deep into a story, to examine all sides, and to play Devil's advocate more often than not.

Rather than tell Kristen how very wrong her

assessment was, Hayley asked, "When does this shindig end, again?"

"At ten." Kristen looked at her watch and then glanced around the room. "We can probably start cleaning up now. The crowd has been filtering out of here for a while."

Then why had she gotten so snide about the cucumbers? Hayley shrugged and followed Kristen's lead.

They pulled a bussing tray out from beneath the table and started putting the older plates of food in it, those that had been sitting out for a while, untouched. They moved the fresher ones to the front of the table and as Hayley crouched to pick up the tray, she remembered she wasn't wearing any panties. The air wafted over her bare flesh and she bit her lip. If only the skirt was longer than just past mid-thigh, but there wasn't much she could do about it now. She certainly didn't have the courage to walk over to her impromptu one-night stand and ask for her underwear back.

So Hayley lifted the tray onto the table, set it on the edge so she could smooth her skirt, and then brought the food back to the kitchen. The staff in the back didn't pay any attention to her. They were also cleaning up from the event, which meant Hayley could just leave the tray and return to her station without anyone even glancing at her.

Still, her cheeks burned at the physical reminder of her unexpected sexual escapade. What had she done or said at the time? What had her expression conveyed that told the woman, "Yes"? She closed her eyes, replaying the scene in her mind.

Hayley had clung to her when they kissed, had offered her tongue, had pulled the woman deeper into the closet with her. In that heady moment, Hayley had been all invitation. As a waitress, having an evening gown-clad woman on her knees in front of her, her face pressed into Hayley's almost-chaste pussy, the moment had made her feel both powerful and ecstatic.

Maybe for the woman, it was some kind of forbidden fantasy, going down on a catering employee. Or maybe there was a connection Hayley had never recognized, even in all their prior interactions at the coffee shop.

Well, shit. She was going to either spend the entire night analyzing it or she was going to get the job done, go back to her noisy dorm, and try to get some sleep.

As she hefted another tray of food off the table and into the kitchen, Hayley decided sleep was unlikely. Not when her body was throbbing, wondering if there was more to come.

Chapter 2

LATE NIGHTS WEREN'T SO BAD, as long as they were a Friday or Saturday because that meant a slightly later morning at the coffee shop. Despite that, Hayley stared blankly at the blender, plastic cup in one hand and flavoring syrup in the other hand.

Coffee was the last thing on her mind. After getting back to her room, she had tossed and turned in bed, trying to forget that woman and their encounter.

But she couldn't. It only made her more aroused if she tried, so she finally gave in to the need to bring herself to orgasm. It wasn't as enjoyable as the one she'd had earlier in the evening, but it alleviated the tension and allowed her to sleep. Still, she just wasn't herself today.

Why was her mind, usually so focused, a million miles away now?

"Yo! Hayley. Get to work. What's with you today?" her boss snapped. He'd been snapping at her all morning and Hayley couldn't blame him. She was definitely out to lunch.

"Sorry." She blinked down at the cup in her hand and tried to remember the order. What was she supposed to be making right now? Her gaze slid to the flavoring syrup in her other hand and she remembered. One of the mocha frappuccinos that was so popular on the menu, of course. Heck, the cup even had "MF" written on it in marker. *Duh.*

It seemed so strange to her that after moving halfway across the country to go to a prestigious school in Washington D.C., she'd learned to tune out the noise of the city and the students, but not her own thoughts. She supposed it would take a very strong person, though, to tune out what had gone down the night before.

"Oh jeez," she sputtered to herself. "Gone down." Shaking her head, Hayley finished layering the ingredients and blending the drink. It wasn't that she usually had dirty thoughts – or even accidentally funny ones – but today appeared to be an exception.

Hayley served up the drink with an apology to the customer and sighed when the manager told her to work the cash register instead. She really didn't want to do that. Really didn't want to see a certain regular customer who would come in as she did every morning to order the exact same thing. But maybe that woman had already come in earlier and missed her.

As Hayley took her place behind the register and looked at the short line of people, she saw one familiar face. It was a face she would never forget, especially after last night.

Shit, Hayley thought, bowing her head and taking a deep breath. That gorgeous woman was in line, tapping away at her mobile phone and smiling in that sensual, mysterious way of hers. The only thing Hayley could do was treat her like just another customer, so she smiled at the next person in line and started taking orders.

She could do this – ignore the heat firing between her legs and spreading that intense warmth throughout the rest of her body. Yes, she could ignore that and focus. Hadn't she spent the past eight years completely focused on what mattered?

When the beautiful blonde's turn came, Hayley put on her best popular coffee-shop chain, "Can I help you?" voice and smile.

"Yes you can, Hayley. In fact, I'd like to be helped

by you every day."

It wasn't the first time they had spoken to each other, but this time Hayley was struck by what the woman's voice sounded like – rich and confident, as though she'd had training in speech or experience with public speaking. She had not just the glamor, but the poise of a Golden Age Hollywood star. Hayley's initial reaction was to shiver at unexpectedly hearing her own name spoken by the woman, but then she remembered she was wearing a nametag.

"I'll take a tall dark roast, please."

The robust coffee a woman like her would prefer, Hayley thought, not quite sure why she was even analyzing it. This was the woman's standard morning order. So many other women came in here for the blended frappuccinos, but not this one. This one had more sophisticated taste.

"What's the name on that?" Hayley asked as she picked up a cup and a marker. Shouldn't she know this by now? Damn, why didn't she?

Because the woman had been just another customer until last night. That's why.

"Veronica."

Hayley printed the name in her small, neat, even letters. Writing was a pure joy to her. She had notebooks and journals from her childhood filled with stories, thoughts, and ideas. Even the act of carefully writing a customer's name on a cup made her feel good. And writing a name as lyrical and pretty as Veronica? She took a little extra time with it, memorizing how creating each letter felt.

After she set the cup aside, she looked up at her customer again. "Can I get you anything else with that today? Scones are two for two dollars."

"Actually, If it wouldn't be too cliché of me to request it, I'd like your phone number." Veronica had lowered her voice and it took on a smoky quality that reignited the fire inside Hayley. "I'd really like to take you to lunch," she clarified. "I feel like we should have a proper date, even though we skipped right past that last night."

"Thank you, but I have to work until five," Hayley answered, looking down at the cash register. Her heartbeat sped up and she wondered if her reaction was giving her away. A tingle rippled along her bare arms, like ice dancing over her skin in response to the heat shooting through her. What kind of answer was that, anyway? Five was the perfect time to get off work and then go to dinner.

Veronica smiled at her. "Five is perfect. A girl's got to eat. Join me for dinner. You won't be disappointed."

Disappointed? The thought that any woman could disappoint her made Hayley want to bark out a laugh, but she held it inside and smiled at the woman. "That's hardly something I'm worried about, but I've got to study after work. No rest for the wicked, you know." Why on earth had she said that? It sounded like she was flirting.

"So you're a student. Finals must be coming up this time of year."

"That's right, they are, so you'll understand why I don't exactly have time to go out. But I appreciate the invitation, Veronica."

Veronica simply held her gaze and her smile didn't falter. "Are you telling me you don't even have time to make friends?" When Hayley shook her head, the woman said, "You must be very devoted to school. Well, it was worth a try, even though I shouldn't have asked anyway."

As Hayley rang up the drink, she furrowed her brow. "What's that supposed to mean?" she asked. Was this because of the obvious difference in their social positions?

"It means several things, but since you've made it clear you're not interested, don't worry about it. At least I tried." Veronica paid and stepped away from the counter, and Hayley glared down at the cup waiting to be filled with dark roast. The cup sat empty, taunting her, within reach, if she really wanted it.

Before anything like her pesky logic or common sense could stop her, Hayley picked up the cup, turned away from the cash register, and scrawled her phone number just below Veronica's name and the "DR." It wasn't the tidiest writing this time, but she'd congratulate Veronica if she could decipher it. She thrust the cup at her manager, who filled the order and handed it off to the customer.

By the time her lunch break rolled around, she hadn't

heard from Veronica, but Hayley remembered she had been wearing one of those short, pleated white skirts and a short-sleeved polo shirt, and carrying a racket under her arm. Veronica would be playing tennis today like a D.C. socialite should. While Hayley? Hayley would be serving coffee to people with disposable income.

Hayley wondered if Veronica played it for fun or fitness. While the idea of any sport didn't appeal to Hayley, she admired the dedication of anyone who took the time to take good care of their body. Especially a body like Veronica's.

"Oh jeez, I need to stop thinking about her," Hayley muttered against her egg-and-cheese sandwich before taking another bite. She was going to spend her break daydreaming the minutes away, instead of doing something constructive. So she pulled out her phone and checked her email again. Still nothing about the interview yet, but she reminded herself it was the weekend.

It wasn't until close to the end of her shift that her phone buzzed with a text notification. Hayley slipped into the bathroom to check it.

If you've changed your mind, let me know and I'll pick you up promptly at 5.

Hayley leaned back against the wall as she stared down at her phone. She was hungry. Lunch had been almost five hours prior. Her stomach let out a rumble at that very moment as if to prove it. But was dinner with a strange woman in a huge city really the solution? Sure, Hayley had lived there for nearly four years, but her life was a strict routine of work and school. No deviation from her plan, the course, she'd charted from college to success.

Still, what could one date hurt?

Hayley heard the bathroom door creak open, followed by a familiar, "Oh, hey you. I swear you're addicted to that phone of yours. No one is emailing about interviews on a Saturday any more than they were last night, for goodness sake." Kristen stepped inside and cocked her head. "And there you go looking kind of weird. Are you all right, Hay? Is something going on or are you just going cuckoo on me with senior year bullshit?"

"Yeah. No. I mean, I'm just tired. We worked late

last night, after all, and I've been here since this morning."

"Right. Yeah. I guess I'd be tired too if I had to get up first thing in the morning and work all day, already." Kristen stepped up to the mirror and checked her makeup. Hayley envied her the evening shift. It wasn't as busy as mornings, but the tips were better in the mornings. She tried to tell herself the money going into her savings account made up for the lack of quality sleep and a social life, but that argument was no longer convincing. Maybe it was senioritis.

Which led her back to her dilemma. She was a senior with only a few weeks left of school. What harm could one little dinner do? Like Kristen kept pointing out, no one was going to send her an important email tonight. Or tomorrow.

Hayley chewed at her lower lip and tapped out her response. It was short but affirmative, and the moment she sent it, her heart raced. She sagged against the wall and tried to catch her breath.

"Are you sure you're doing okay?" Kristen turned and watched her. "I think the pressure is getting to you.

Seriously."

"No, it's not there. I'm fine. I just said yes to a date."

"A date? You?" Now the expression of concern on Kristen's face turned to disbelief. "You accepted a date? Is that what this is all about – some babe? I've known you for almost four years now and you haven't dated except... Gosh, what was her name? Elena something in freshman year. Now I'm definitely worried. Who are you and what have you done with Hayley? You know who I mean – that girl who studies all the time, instead of having fun – where did that girl go?"

"Come on, Kristen. I'm serious and a little freaked out."

"Sure you are." Kristen widened her eyes and put her hands over her mouth. "Oh, you are! Who is she? Is she one of the journalism students or does she have a different major?"

Hayley gently bit her tongue as she mulled over her answer. What did she know about Veronica besides the fact that she liked dark roast and had a voice that could melt butter? "I'm pretty sure she's not a student. She's probably not even affiliated with the college. I've never seen her there, anyway."

"Intriguing. So how do you know her?"

"Well, I wouldn't say I know her." Hayley watched as her phone screen faded to black. "She's a regular customer here."

"Even more intriguing. Are you really dating one of the customers? If it doesn't work out, are you just going to spit in her coffee?"

Hayley felt ill at the thought. "That's juvenile and disgusting. It's just one date, so if it doesn't work, that's fine. She can just stay a customer, no harm done."

"Speaking of customers, we better get out there. Mike seems kind of pissed. Have you been acting like this all day?"

"I'm afraid so. Just a sec." The phone buzzed and Hayley thumbed over it to pull up the notification. Veronica's text confirmed the date and Hayley sagged even harder against the wall. They'd made plans for less than forty-five minutes from now. There was no turning back.

Hayley let out a low groan as she caught sight of herself in the mirror and Kristen followed her gaze. "Are you going out right after work?" the other girl asked.

"Yeah…"

"Here." Kristen dug around in her purse. She was a one-woman cosmetic shop and now she pulled out a brush, powder, mascara, and lipstick. "Let's at least make you look a little more presentable since your Princess Charming will be here in thirty minutes."

After Kristen's handiwork, Hayley looked more put-together, but she didn't feel more confident.

The rest of her shift passed in a haze. Hayley tidied up the shop, wiping down tables and refilling napkin holders. But the entire time, she wasn't focused on her work. All she could think about was the fact that she was about to face a woman who was her first and only one-night stand. Then again, calling their encounter a one-night stand was generous. It had been more like a fifteen-minute stand. Fifteen minutes of standing against a wall while the most glamorous woman she had ever seen pleasured her. Fifteen minutes that changed her life and turned the direction of her thoughts upside down.

For the first time in four years, she was thinking about doing something fun. After eschewing anything that didn't bring her closer to her goal, she was stepping just a little bit out of her comfort zone and trying something different. What was it about Veronica that made Hayley decide to do this?

Her thoughts returned to the idea of senioritis. She couldn't spend her entire youth focused on work, work, work, she decided. Once in a while, she had to let herself have a little fun.

So she put away the cleaning cloths and bundles of napkins, hung up her apron, clocked out, and picked up her things. When she looked at the front door, there was Veronica, looking poised and beautiful.

Waiting for her with a smug smile.

Chapter 3

"WHAT?" HAYLEY SHRUNK A bit in her chair. It already made her feel uncomfortable that she was in a posh restaurant wearing jeans and a plain black t-shirt. She didn't have any time to change between work and the date. At least Veronica wasn't too dressed up, either, but her black slacks and peach-colored shirt were at least more elegant-looking than Hayley's casual barista ensemble.

Veronica leaned forward and covered one side of her mouth as she asked softly, "Are you all right? You look a little uncomfortable."

"Um, yeah. No." Hayley glanced around the restaurant. The dim lights and soft music were almost as disconcerting as her memory of Veronica going down on her at the gala. She thought she'd left awkward after-sex moments behind her when she decided to focus on school, but clearly not. "I feel like… well, I'm not sure why we're here."

"Oh dear. Not much for following your heart or indulging in a little spontaneity, are you?" The expression on Veronica's face was mischievous, far too playful for Hayley's liking. "Well, except for very special moments."

Without meaning to, Hayley glared at her. "Is this some kind of weird game of yours – forbidden sex with a blue-collar stranger in a semi-public place, followed by asking them to dinner? It seems a little backward to me."

"Yes, but you were just as enthusiastic about that night as I was, so…" Veronica's shoulders relaxed and she nodded. "I guess I should start with explanations, then. The appetizers here are amazing. Let's get the spinach dip."

Hayley compressed her lips and looked at Veronica. "How can you go from offering an explanation to spinach dip? I would just really appreciate it if we clarify things. Is this a date?"

"On the record, maybe. Off the record, yes, I would like it to be. Does that work for you?"

"I don't know. What's with this on-the-record, off-the-record stuff?" Those were journalism terms and Hayley couldn't figure out why the heck Veronica was using them.

A pensive expression crossed Veronica's face and she leaned back in her chair, folded her arms, and stared at Hayley. "You don't know who I am, do you?"

"You're Veronica. You order a dark roast every morning and..." Hayley cleared her throat. The words *You're the most beautiful woman I've ever seen* nearly tripped off the end of her tongue, but she simply concluded, "And you just happened to be at a party I was working last night."

"Interesting." The smile returned to Veronica's face and she lowered her slim, elegant hands to the menu. "Well, then, I recommend the shrimp scampi if you like seafood."

"Thanks." Hayley looked over the menu and when the waitress took their orders, went with Veronica's recommendation. But her head was spinning the entire time. How did she do that – just shift from one topic to another, and so smoothly? Unlike normal people, Veronica didn't "um" or "ah." She didn't giggle awkwardly. Her mannerisms were graceful and almost too perfect.

After the waitress collected the menus and gave them

a basket of breadsticks, Veronica placed her hands on the table and said, "I want you to know I noticed you when you first started working at the coffee shop. That's where this all begins."

"You did?" Hayley hesitated as she reached for the basket. She was just a college student working a barista job for some extra money. There was certainly nothing extraordinary or worth noticing about that.

"Mmhm, but I guess you didn't notice me beyond associating my face with my coffee choice. I think I've spent the last six months really thinking about you, Hayley, trying to figure out how to get your attention. I understand why you just thought of me as another customer. It's not like you ever gave me any indication that you were interested in me. Every day, I got your 'May I help you?' smile and something about it..." Veronica shrugged and grinned at her. "Anyway, I'm a sucker for cute, wholesome, and Midwestern."

"How do you know I'm Midwestern?" Hayley asked. She thought about the few high school girlfriends she'd had. Those experiences had been less about physical attraction and more about being the only lesbians within twenty miles of each other. That and confirming that they definitely were not attracted to boys, followed by satisfying their adolescent curiosity about sex.

"Well, it doesn't take psychic powers to figure it out. First of all, I've rubbed elbows with people from all over the country. Well, all over the world, really, so I can identify a Midwestern accent. Though I'm a little hazy on which state, I'd guess somewhere smack-dab in the middle of the U.S. Probably Nebraska. Maybe Colorado, but you don't seem worldly enough for that. Colorado is a pretty hip place, so I'm guessing you're a Cornhusker State girl – wholesome, friendly, no BS, no pretension, honest, and hard working. Am I right?"

Hayley blinked several times and blew out a breath that lifted her bangs. How did Veronica do that?

"I nailed it, didn't I?" Veronica asked. "You have that wonderful, friendly vibe Nebraskans give off. Anyway, I thought you were cute and even though you didn't give off the vibe, I thought it was worth asking you out. Then you were working the party last night and…" Veronica shrugged as if there was nothing more to say.

"Yeah, I guess that's where you really lose me, actually." Hayley looked down at the table. It seemed like each time she recalled the previous night, her cheeks got hot and her entire face flushed. Whether that was because of the casual sex or the taboo way they went about it, she wasn't quite sure yet. "I mean, why didn't you just talk to me, like ask me out at the coffee shop the way you did today?"

"Why didn't I?" Veronica echoed. She fluttered her eyelashes in a way that would look ridiculous on any other woman, but on Veronica it was charming. "I followed you back there last night to talk to you, but there was something about that moment that I couldn't resist. You were so cute in your waitressing uniform, I was there in my best evening gown, and the idea of letting the opportunity pass me by was too much. I had to kiss you."

Hayley let out a snort. "You did more than kiss me."

"True, but you kissed back."

"I couldn't help it." It was a confession Hayley didn't know if she should make, but she prided herself on her honesty.

Now a triumphant look crossed Veronica's face. "I know. The way you kissed me back, I could tell it'd been a while. So I thought I'd take a chance."

"Yeah, but how did you know I'd go for it?" Hayley asked. As far as she knew, she didn't give off any sort of "vibe" that she was gay, let alone up for anything sexual. Maybe Veronica saw something in her that Hayley didn't. She certainly seemed astute at figuring people out.

"Lucky guess, I suppose. You melted in my arms and that was that." Veronica shrugged, the nonchalant gesture letting Hayley know she was the kind of person who lived in the moment.

Hayley wondered what it was like to be so carefree, to be able to do whatever one felt at the time. From the time she was a child, she'd been nothing like that. It probably didn't help that her only way to achieve her dreams was having strict enough discipline to see her ambitions through.

Veronica seemed to be scrutinizing her or aware of the direction of her thoughts, because she asked, "You're not much for giving into feelings, are you?"

"Not when they don't get me where I need to be, no."

"That's very pragmatic of a Midwesterner and if there's one thing you guys are known for, it's pragmatism." Veronica looked around the restaurant. "But here in the big D.C., people do things a little differently. Ambition is something you have to mask and sometimes even ration. Keeping your thoughts and intentions close to the vest is a smarter move than, say, letting someone know what you want when you want it."

When her gaze fastened on Hayley again, Hayley felt her heartbeat pick up. "What do you mean by that?" she asked.

"I mean I've lived here a long time and I know how to play the game. Even been coached by the best on how to do it. I can teach you those rules too."

"Rules. I prefer rules," Hayley said with a nod. She liked parameters and limits. They kept everything in order.

"I'll bet you do, because they keep things organized and structured, and I know you're an organized and structured girl. But…" Veronica leaned forward and winked at her. "These rules are going to be harder for you to play by if you feel like you always need to speak your mind and do what's right."

Hayley smoothed out the wince that threatened to crease her brow. "What do you mean by that?" she asked. "How can there be rules without them being perfectly straightforward?"

"Ah, our plucky heroine wants to know how to survive in the shark tank." Veronica sat back in her seat and smiled up at the waitress who served the food. It was the first thing Hayley realized she had noticed about Veronica – that smile. It was wide and sincere and dazzling, and she used it anytime, anywhere. Just that quirk of Veronica's lips made the corners of her eyes crinkle and that's when Hayley also realized Veronica was probably much older than her. Older than she had initially guessed.

"Why do you call this a shark tank?" Hayley asked after the waitress left their table. Bringing up their ages at this time seemed pointless, so she let the thought go and focused on the plate in front of her. The food smelled amazing – like a mixture of garlic and oregano –

and she couldn't wait to taste it.

"Please. Have you not been watching the news since, I don't know, forever?"

Of course she had. Ever since she was in middle school, Hayley had been fascinated by everything that went on, not just in her own country, but around the world. "I have, yes. Life is being lived everywhere every day, and I'm always curious about the impacts on people and the ultimate mark left on history."

"Interesting response. If you feel that way, you'll learn fast that no one here cares about your wide-eyed dreams. All they care about is getting ahead. They don't talk about it, though. You can't tell your co-worker you're going for this promotion or that opportunity. The more you keep quiet, the more likely you are to advance. That is rule number one."

"Excuse me, but I'm not going into journalism just to 'get ahead'," Hayley pointed out, bitterness lacing her tone. "I'm here to tell people the truth about what's happening in our world."

"Like Woodward and Bernstein? Oh, darling." Veronica shook her head. "You think you left the

Midwest to make a difference, to get away from the same ol', same ol' every day, and do something noble. Yet here you are, living the same routine day after day. I bet you go to school and work, and do nothing in between, other than study and sleep. And for what? To get in on the ground floor of a job that represents a romantic notion of the past."

Even though the food tasted incredible, Hayley felt it turn to ashes in her mouth. "That's harsh," she said after swallowing her first bite, "not to mention cynical."

"Ah, but true. I bet you want to work for a newspaper, but newspapers are a dying breed, my dear. Trust me. I know. I was born in this town. I'll probably die in this town, but not before the newspapers."

"And what makes you an expert on the media?" Hayley asked, stabbing at her scampi with her fork. "Do you work for a newspaper?"

Veronica half-smiled this time as she twirled her pasta with her fork. "No."

"Do your parents?"

This time she laughed, a low, almost mocking sound. "Darling, my father would rather shoot a reporter than look at him. But don't worry – I don't share his sentiments. You're safe with me."

"Look, I appreciate the dinner and the warning, but I'm not sure what the point of all of this is. I thought this was a date. Are you just playing some kind of weird game with me?" Exasperation and confusion made Hayley's heart race. Here she was, just a normal college student, preparing for her life after graduation, and this woman was speaking in riddles.

"Sorry. I forgot you don't have the guile so many of the insiders do. It's been a long time since I sat down with someone who wasn't interested in what they wanted to hear me say, but what I actually have to say." Veronica traced her finger around her wineglass. "Hayley, you're not like other women I've met and I want to get to know you better."

"Why?"

"Well, why does anyone lust after anyone else? Who knows? And why does anyone fall in love? Scientists have worked on these questions for years and it seems to come down to chemical reactions but, again…" Veronica shrugged. "The point is, I feel drawn to you and not just for a fling. Despite the fact that I shouldn't even consider dating, especially publicly, I feel like you're someone I can take a chance on. You have that whole earnest thing going on. It's adorable."

Adorable. Like she was some kind of kitten who had lost her way and not an ambitious, driven college student about to graduate and take her next steps in life. "I'm not a pet," Hayley shot back as she watched Veronica take a bite of pasta.

"Not yet, but I've always wanted one."

"That's not funny."

Veronica rolled her eyes. "It was a joke, doll, and you're right. Forgive me?"

"I'll forgive you if you stop calling me 'honey' and 'darling' and 'doll.' Look, I'm sure you're used to..." Hayley flailed her hands helplessly in Veronica's direction. "How you are, but I don't like it. You don't need to put on your little charming socialite act for me. Just cut the crap. It's not working."

For a moment, Veronica compressed her lips and stared at her. Now there was a hard gleam in her eye, but it softened a moment later. "I'm not used to people calling me on my shit."

"Yeah, well, privilege does that to a person. You're also probably not used to living in a rickety two-bedroom house that'd be better described as a shack, or not seeing your parents all day long because they're working their asses off on the farm. And I certainly bet you're not used to working your own ass off on weekends and nights since you were fourteen, just to save money for something that matters to you, even though you know you've got all the scholarships you need to cover it, and then moving across the country to chase a dream, only to have some snooty bitch mock it."

"No, I'm not and I don't know what it's like." Veronica looked apologetic, but Hayley spoke up before she could say anything else.

"Don't apologize. You waltzed into that supply closet like you knew you were going to get what you wanted and then you thought I'd just fall into your arms after that. Well, maybe I did have a moment of weakness and I don't feel bad about that. I needed it because you're right – I work damn hard for something that might not even be a logical goal, considering how media is changing. But you know what? It's *my* goal and the only person who gets to dictate how I should live my life is me." Hayley folded her arms and glared down at her food, not sure she wanted it anymore.

"Jeez." Veronica bowed her head and placed her hands over her face. The way her shoulders hunched surprised Hayley. Considering Veronica's usual swagger, she seemed unsinkable. Then again, anything proclaimed unsinkable usually proved the opposite to be true.

Hayley was relieved when Veronica smoothed her hands back over her blonde hair and looked up at her with a watery smile.

"I'm making a terrible second impression."

"Yes, you are," Hayley agreed.

"And you deserve better than that."

"I do, but it's too late now." Hayley rose from her seat and reached into her purse. She tossed thirty dollars on the table, hoping it would cover her dinner, drink, and tip. "Thank you anyway," she said and left the restaurant.

Despite the protest in Veronica's eyes, the other

woman didn't say a word to her, which suited Hayley
just fine. By the time she was back at her dorm, she
decided she could just let the event go down in history as
a bad date and forget about it.

She tossed and turned in bed, though, as she
remembered there was no forgetting Veronica.

First of all, she was a regular customer at the coffee
shop. Second...

Was there a second? Hayley supposed there was. She
certainly couldn't forget that scorching meeting at the
hotel during the gala. But they were both going to have
to let it go, she decided. Maybe Veronica would be too
ashamed to face her and avoid the coffee shop or find
another one for her morning caffeine fix.

Since Hayley couldn't just drop her job on a whim,
she hoped Veronica would acknowledge the logic of
simply going to a different shop and leave her alone, or
at least pretending they didn't know each other. It
seemed like the best solution, but Hayley already knew
what Veronica thought of reason and logic.

It didn't look promising for her.

Chapter 4

"MAKE-UP COFFEE?" HAYLEY stared at Veronica over the cash register. "Life isn't like school. It's not like a test you tried hard on and failed. You can't just make it up. Seriously. Just order something and leave."

Of course, Veronica hadn't given up. Hayley wanted to ask her what was wrong with her, but she stood her ground and waited for an answer.

"Fine, maybe coffee is a bad idea. I'm sure you're coffeed out, anyway."

"Coffeed isn't an adjective. It's not even a word." Hayley was grateful that Sunday mornings at the coffee shop were slow because the last thing she wanted was an audience as Veronica tried to convince her to give her another chance.

Veronica had the grace to look chagrined. "Fine, you're the linguistics expert, while I'm just a useless playgirl with too much time on her hands. How about a walk, then. There's a beautiful park not far from here. Or we could visit something meaningful, like the Washington Monument."

A walk. Now that *was* an appealing idea, Hayley had to admit. If there was one thing she missed about small-town life, it was things like picnics and festivals, and open spaces where she could walk and just enjoy getting fresh air. It had been a chance to pretend she wasn't so poor, to meander and dream, and appreciate her close-knit community. More often than not, Hayley would bring her little sister along, while her parents put in long hours – as usual – over the weekend. Besides, she couldn't ask their elderly neighbor to keep an eye on her sister all the time and her parents were so grateful when she handled things herself.

How could someone like Veronica understand any of this about her? Granted, Hayley knew nothing about Veronica and she really didn't want to, either. But it seemed like Veronica wasn't willing to let their connection go without a fight.

And Hayley had to admit she felt a connection. Just seeing Veronica made her heart leap with excitement, which only exacerbated the frustration in her mind. When she imagined her love life in the future…

Well, she didn't really think of it at all, but she

figured she would fall in love with a fellow workaholic journalist. Probably a woman she saw in passing more often than not. Maybe they would share an apartment, share a coffee cup in the morning in their haste to get dressed, accidentally swap briefcases, and all the things romantic comedy movies were made of.

Veronica was straight out of a terrible high school dramedy about queen bees and the studious good girls they liked to torment.

"You've been here since probably opening, right?" Veronica asked.

"Yeah," Hayley answered shortly. She hated how perceptive Veronica was when it came to her and she had to restrain herself from fiddling with the cash register as an outlet for her frustration. The last thing she wanted was for Veronica to see that she got to her.

"So now that it's going on eleven, I bet you're hungry and your lunch break is probably coming up soon."

Actually, Hayley was going to get off work at eleven, but she wasn't sure she should tell Veronica that. She usually used Sunday afternoons to treat herself to a special lunch, catch up on email, look over her planner, assess her work for the week, and then read a book until she went to bed. It was an essential weekly ritual that made her feel like she had at least some control over the constant go-go-go of her life. Sunday was her down day – five hours of work, followed by nineteen hours of rest.

She supposed a walk with Veronica, especially if they could pick up a salad or healthy sandwich, would count as a special lunch and if things went as well as they did last night, it certainly wouldn't be a long lunch.

"My shift ends at eleven," Hayley admitted. She had nothing to lose. Except for maybe another ounce of her already fraying sanity.

"Great. I'll get everything together. I'll be back."

"What do you mean by 'everything'?" Hayley asked.

"You'll see." Veronica winked at her, turned on her heel, and strutted out of the coffee shop.

Hayley watched as Veronica left. As soon as the blonde turned the corner, Hayley leaned against the counter and sighed. What had she just done? Was she a masochist for agreeing to a second date, when the first one had ended so abruptly? Or did she feel whatever it was that Veronica felt – a compulsion to be around her?

"Clearly I'm just an idiot," Hayley muttered against her palms as she turned away from the cash register and scrubbed her hands over her face.

Still, that idiocy did come with fresh air and stretching her legs on a gorgeous, warm day.

Thirty minutes later, they were perched on the edge of the Bartholdi Fountain, eating wraps and sipping from water bottles. Hayley had to admit she appreciated Veronica's efforts to put a nice lunch together while keeping it casual. This was a much more comfortable setting than the swanky restaurant from the previous night.

"So, why Georgetown University?" Veronica asked as she crossed her legs at the ankles, a pose that seemed at odds with her sensual, outgoing personality, as far as Hayley was concerned. Veronica seemed more like the femme fatale, the sort to cross her legs at the knees and then open them at inappropriate moments. Hayley tried to shove thoughts of Sharon Stone's character in *Basic Instinct* out of her mind.

"How did you know I go there?" Hayley tucked a

strand of hair behind her ear and barely restrained herself from taking a huge bite of her chicken wrap. It was her favorite food – light, tasty, and easy to eat on the go.

"Hayley Becker, how hard do you think it is to learn about you?" With a giggle, Veronica crumpled her already-empty sandwich paper and shoved it into a small plastic bag. "Let's just say I have my ways."

This time Hayley let out a derisive snort. "Please. Google isn't that much of a secret. Even we simple Midwesterners know that."

"First of all, I never called you 'simple.' I called you wholesome. And second, no, it's not, but that's not the only thing I have at my disposal." Veronica looked at her and grinned. "Did you Google me?"

"No," Hayley answered and took another bite of her wrap.

"Come on, I bet you did."

Hayley shook her head. She wasn't going to wait any longer, especially if Veronica was going to get into some cat-and-mouse game with her.

"Well, then. Some reporter you are."

"What's that supposed to mean?"

"No fact gathering on your part. How hard would it have been to find me?"

"Considering I don't know your last name..." Hayley shrugged as she devoured the last bite of her wrap. There was no sense in drawing out their meeting. Veronica seemed hell-bent on more cat-and-mouse BS.

While Hayley stuffed the wrapping in the bag Veronica gave to her, Veronica pulled out her phone and tapped at the screen with her thumbs. "There. I just entered 'Veronica' and 'Washington D.C.' Why don't you tell me if you could find anything on me without my last name."

Hayley looked at the phone Veronica had turned her way and her eyes widened. On the front page of Google, there were several images across the top, all of Veronica. A couple

were professional photos, but the rest looked like red carpet-style photos, some solo and some with a much older, dignified-looking man at her side.

"So that's you. Veronica Stone-McClusky." Hayley looked up at her. "You're married?"

"No. I just used to use the McClusky name when I

was younger because of the doors it opened for me. But now I prefer to use my mother's name because of reasons." As usual when she made some sort of vague statement, Veronica was grinning at her maddeningly, like she was playing a game or expected Hayley to figure out what she meant.

Now it was Hayley's turn to do her best to feign nonchalance as she handed the phone back to Veronica. "So you're a big deal and apparently your father is, too."

"Political science definitely wasn't your thing, but you're going to need to brush up on our government before you even set one toe into the *Washington Post* building," Veronica said, shaking her head and sliding her phone back into her purse. "That is, of course, if you want to report on Washington politics. Otherwise, you better go back to the newspaper farm league."

"What's that supposed to mean?"

"First of all, if you're a reporter, you need to learn to dig and investigate. The facts won't just come to you. Second, know the town you plan to work in, babe."

"I know all of that. I worked at the paper at the University," Hayley grumbled, indignation warming her from head to toe.

"Which one?"

"The Georgetown Voice."

"Nice. So back to my original question – what brought you to Georgetown University?"

Hayley took a sip of water as she considered the question. "Well, first I had to find a place where I could learn about journalism and I really wanted to do it in the heart of Washington D.C. since, yes, I would like to work for the *Washington Post*. And then I wanted a place where I would have new experiences and diversity. And then I had to make sure it was a place I could afford with the scholarships I got. Even though I have to take journalism as a minor to get my bachelor's degree, going somewhere like Georgetown was part of the dream."

"Afford? Afford a college."

"Yeah, why not?" Since Veronica was looking at her in disbelief, Hayley knew the only way to keep the ball rolling was to explain herself. "Look, I got a full ride and all just for acing the ACT and the SAT, but I felt bad asking for the scholarships to pay for some kind of expensive, Ivy League college. And even with the scholarships, I've worked eight hours a day since I was fourteen just so I could save money for and after college."

"Did you manage to save enough money to go to college for all four years?"

"I did, yeah. I didn't have to use all of it because I got the academic scholarships. But yeah – I saved up over a hundred thousand dollars working seven days a week, eight hours a day."

Veronica compressed her lips and glared at her. "That should be illegal for a minor to work so much."

"Well, where I'm from, it's perfectly legal for a teenager to work eight hours a day. I had two different jobs, of course, but it was worth it. I've kept on working, lived frugally the past four years, and everything has worked out. Instead of graduating in debt, I'll graduate with enough money to start my life."

"Uh-huh, but you're exhausted and never have any fun. That doesn't sound like something to brag about."

Hayley capped her water and tried not to imagine what it would be like to throw it in Veronica's perfect face. They had chemistry, all right, the kind that made

Hayley seethe with frustration. "I suppose your life is nothing like that, Ms. I Use My Mother's Maiden Name. You never had to earn a thing in your life, right?"

"Most definitely not. Granted, I'm not exactly proud of my father, but I managed to make my own living without him, at least."

"Why aren't you proud of your father?" Now it sounded like Veronica had something juicy and interesting to say about herself, but the other woman shut her down with a wave of her hand.

"Anyway, I followed in my mother's footsteps and I'm glad I did." Veronica gave her another of those dazzling smiles that made Hayley forget there was a huge gulf between them, both socially and economically. In that moment, she didn't want to be wholesome Hayley anymore. She wanted Veronica to slide right up next to her and kiss her.

How the hell could Hayley's intense dislike turn to lust like that, in zero to sixty seconds? Maybe scientists could explain that one of these days.

But she shook that thought out of her head and asked, "What does your mother do?"

"Now that I've demonstrated the power of Google to you, I'm sure you can figure it out for yourself. Let's just enjoy this beautiful day." Veronica seemed to have closed the subject because she sat there drinking her water and giving Hayley an occasional half-smile.

Hayley said, "Well, I would, but I think it's time to get going. I better get back to the dorms and get some work done."

"Work? What do you mean work?"

"Work is that thing we plebeians have to do every day to keep moving ahead in life since we weren't born there."

"Aw, stay. It's a gorgeous day. And just look at the view – have you even taken the time to see the sights here?"

Hayley looked back at the beautiful old fountain and suppressed a sigh. No, she hadn't taken the time to tour her nation's capital. How ridiculous was that? She'd come here with a passion for knowledge and sharing information with others, but hadn't actually seen the city she'd called home for four years and planned to live in for the rest of her life.

"Don't tell me you came here for college and haven't been on the National Mall or toured the White House or seen the Lincoln Memorial."

Hayley knew her shrug told all, but she added a "Nope" to the gesture.

"Oh, that just isn't right. You have to let me be your tour guide."

"No." Hayley tucked her hair behind her ears as she shook her head. "I don't have time for that."

"Of course you do! You're about to graduate. This is the time to blow off classes and party it up!"

"No, this is the time to get job interviews scheduled."

Veronica waved her hand. "Please. Don't be so serious. You said so yourself – you have over a hundred grand saved up to start your life. Cut yourself some slack."

"Some of us can't afford not to be serious. Do you know how easy it is to spend a hundred grand on living expenses?" Hayley pushed herself to her feet. Her heart was racing and now getting a kiss from Veronica was the last thing on her mind. "You know what? I think we're done with this dating thing. It's obvious this isn't going to work out. We're too different and you aren't willing to let me get to know you, to see another side of you that might make me change my mind. So thank you for the lunch and I'll see you around."

"Really? Why are we too different? Is it because I'm trying to get you to have a little fun in your life?"

"Partly. I mean, we have nothing in common – nothing whatsoever – and here you are just being a huge pain in my butt. And for what? If you're just looking for a good time, I'm sorry, but I'm not the girl for you." Hayley turned, but Veronica called to her when she was only a few steps away.

Hayley turned back and folded her arms as Veronica approached her. "Look, I was serious when I told you I like you. I know I'm hard to be around and I'm sorry about that." Veronica actually looked contrite.

"I appreciate that, but we have nothing in common. I think we're better off as acquaintances. But you're interesting and it was very nice meeting you. Now if you'll excuse me, I need to get home."

Chapter 5

AFTER SHE GOT BACK to her dorm room, Hayley couldn't think. She tried turning up her favorite Dar Williams CD and spreading out her work in front of her all over the bed like she usually did on a Sunday afternoon. She chose her bed because it kept her from giving into the temptation to check her computer. Even as she flipped through her planner, though, she couldn't stop glancing at her computer.

Maybe Veronica was right about her – she was slacking off on the info gathering. No journalist would let something as interesting as the mystery of Veronica pass them by. Would they? When Hayley had worked at her high school newspaper and at *The Georgetown Voice*, she had been relentless in her pursuit of facts. It had mattered to her even more once she got to the college newspaper. Impressing her editor-in-chief was of the utmost importance and getting front-page features looked great in her portfolio. This was the kind of work that got a grad hired at the *Washington Post*.

She glanced again over her shoulder at her computer.

"Fine," she told herself. "Let's see what I can dig up because..." Then she swallowed, rather than continue to speak aloud. She knew why she was doing it and it wasn't just journalistic curiosity.

It wasn't long before Google helped her connect the dots about Veronica. The professional photos were modeling headshots and at least seventy-five percent of the hits on her were from fashion magazines before 2015.

A model. That surprised Hayley, but it didn't shock her.

But the other twenty-five percent of hits made Hayley cringe. It was no wonder Veronica wanted to distance herself from her father. Hayley bit her lip and wondered if she had dodged a bullet by telling Veronica they were done dating. The last person she wanted to connect herself with was the daughter of a politician whose stance on social issues wasn't just right-wing, but oppressive.

That still left Veronica's supposed attraction to her unexplained, but Hayley decided that didn't matter anymore. Sure, Veronica was hot and good – *really good*

– at sex. Sure, she kept Hayley on her toes, which was a nice change of pace from being around college students and professors all the time. And, yeah, Hayley felt a tingle shoot through her body from just thinking about Veronica. She didn't even need to picture her on her knees in that evening gown, her tongue lapping at Hayley in a semi-public storage room.

No, no, no.

No, it didn't matter. All that mattered was working toward her future. She needed a job. There was no way she was giving up her dream. One of these days, she was going home and showing everyone what they expected – the small town girl had done well for herself. And how proud her parents would be...

Thinking of home was all it took for Hayley to regain her focus and get back to her usual routine. As she settled back on her bed with her planner and various assignments for the week, her phone buzzed. Picking it up, she swiped the notification icon. Her heart hammered in her chest. It was her email.

They wanted to schedule an interview.

It was a Sunday afternoon, but they had emailed to

see if she would be available sometime in the next week.
Yes!

✳✳✳

A couple of days later, Hayley walked out of the
Washington Post building not sure if she should feel
confident or worried. She certainly wasn't the only
fresh-faced, apprehensive college senior sitting in the
waiting room, knees locked together and hands placed
atop them. The sheer number of interviewees was
concerning. But once she was in the conference room
with the interviewer, she felt better. One-on-one, she was
able to relax a little and focus on giving her elevator
pitch. The interviewer seemed impressed with her
knowledge and portfolio of articles. Now it was just a
matter of waiting to see if she got a second interview.

There was one person Hayley could think of who
would help her make sense of it and as soon as she got
back to her dorm, she'd have to see if she could find her.
But when she opened her door, she was surprised to see
the very person she had in mind sitting at her desk,
typing away on a tablet.

"Elise," she said as she walked into the room and

shut the door behind her. It wasn't often that her suite mate graced her with her presence. Elise knew and respected Hayley's routines, but she also was the only person Hayley had told about today's interview. "Hey, I was hoping to talk to you."

"Well, I thought you could use some support." Elise Shaw had flawless, dark skin and wore her shoulder-length black hair straight. Her long, graceful fingers flew across her tablet keyboard with ease. "Just one... sec..."

Hayley set her purse and portfolio on the bed and stretched as she crossed the room. Crouching in front of the refrigerator, she took a deep breath.

Finally, she was in a safe space where she could reflect on the interview and everything else going on in her life. In a way, the fact that she was always working kept her from having to think about those things. For the past four years, her life had been a series of jobs and goals, with very little time for self-reflection. Now that her academics were easing up a bit, things had slowed down. Even with the pressure to schedule interviews, Hayley found herself with a little more time on her hands than usual. Not much, but enough that she had to find new ways to fill it.

"There." Elise closed her tablet and spun in the chair. "That's the last article I ever have to write for *The Georgetown Voice*. It's the end of an era. I'm not sure if I should cry or celebrate."

"Yeah, I know what you mean. Life is weird like that right now. I think we should celebrate after finals next week. Do you want a pop?"

"Soda, girl. It's soda here on the east coast. And yes, please." Elise took the can Hayley offered her and grinned at her. "So, tell me everything. Was the *Washington Post* everything you expected?"

"It was all that and more." Hayley sank back on her bed and sipped at her can of soda. "Gosh, it would be so exciting to work there. The hustle and bustle, and writing about important things, things that matter. Can you see me at one of those desks, frantically meeting deadlines?"

Elise nodded and tapped the top of her can. "I can see that, yeah. But you know you can always come with me to the *Feminist Flag*. I know the *Washington Post* is your dream newspaper, but digital media is the hot thing now. The *Flag* is looking for smart writers who give a shit about the issues, too, and their readership is constantly growing."

Hayley couldn't deny that the idea was tempting. She believed deeply in the same causes as Elise and she knew most people got their news online. But there was something deeply moving about the idea of working for a paper like the *Washington Post*, a newspaper with a history.

"I do want to write about those issues," she said, "but I hope having a wider audience will give them a louder voice."

"All voices matter, even if you have a smaller forum. Being louder doesn't mean people will listen to you, though. Voices like yours and mine will help reach others. I still love the idea of us carrying on our column from *The Georgetown Voice*. *Feminist Flag* would love it – the black and white perspectives, and how we can work together for a common cause, by addressing the things people are afraid to discuss."

"Honestly, I would love it too," Hayley answered, "but I just have to give the *Washington Post* a chance first, see if they'll give me a chance, you know?"

Her friend rolled her eyes. "Fine, I won't stand in the way of your childhood dreams, but don't forget me when you become a famous journalist busting stuff like the Watergate scandal wide open."

"Please. You're a better writer than I am. More insightful and much sharper." Hayley finished her soda and set it on the dresser next to the foot of her bed. "Speaking of which, maybe you can answer a question for me."

"Go for it."

Figuring out how to phrase the question was the easy part. Hayley just hoped Elise wouldn't dig for more, as was her nature. "Why do you think a person is attracted to another person who is their complete opposite?"

Elise hummed thoughtfully and moved her tablet from her lap to Hayley's desk. "Is this a facetious question or do you have a personal reason for asking it?"

She should have known Elise would dig a bit, but Hayley couldn't help but respond honestly. "Personal reason," she clarified. "I've been dating a little bit, and it seems right and wrong at the same time if that makes sense."

"Well, then, I guess it depends on the people. It being you, I suppose you're talking about a woman."

Hayley nodded once.

"And clearly you like her despite the fact that she is very different than you."

"Actually, it seems to be the opposite. She has a thing for me, but I don't really like her." Even as she said the words, Hayley knew she was lying to both Elise and herself. She had to come clean, at least just to hear herself say the words. "Let me rephrase that. I don't really like her, but I lust after her. I can't get her out of my mind and it's frustrating."

Elise's laugh was rich and throaty, and she shook her head. "You, little miss self-control, lust after someone? I'm surprised, but this is probably a good thing for you."

"Go ahead and laugh at me, but I'm not immune to human emotions."

"Everything I know about you contradicts that." Elise leaned back and propped her elbow on the desk. "You're all about the job, getting it done. Never once have you pointed out a chick you found attractive, yet you've put up with me always pointing out guys, telling you I think they're hot."

It was true and Hayley knew it. She'd gone through college pretty much celibate, except for a few freshman flings. It wasn't that she didn't want to have sex. Heck, she loved sex, as she found out in high school. It was just that pursuing her goals left little time, let alone desire, for anything fun. And then there was the question of intimacy. How could she have that in her life when her life revolved around the dream of a career?

"Anyway, I'm going to guess you lust after this person *because* they're so different than you. Not despite it."

Damn, Elise was good.

"That makes sense, but why does she like me?" Hayley asked.

"Is that harder for you to understand?"

"Yeah. I mean, she's…" Hayley shifted on the bed and tried to think of how to explain Veronica. "She's posh and perfect and, I don't know, a little bit scary."

Elise laughed again. "Okay, okay, you have to explain 'scary' because I'm intrigued."

"Oh gosh." Hayley covered her face with her hands.

It wasn't often that she reacted physically to anything. She didn't blush or fidget, didn't bite her lip or twirl her hair – didn't do any of the things so many other young women did when they were put off-kilter. But she knew if she wasn't careful, she would give away too much with just the wrong words.

Then again, Elise was her best friend here at school. She was smart and probably discreet. Hayley blew out a long breath as she uncovered her face.

"She's just someone who really knows what she wants and isn't afraid to chase it."

"So, she's just like you after all," Elise said.

"Well, yeah, in a way. Only she doesn't do it because she's passionate about something. She does it because she's rich and spoiled, and used to getting everything to go her way. And I'm just not sure I can deal with that. She's also older than me and super savvy about living in D.C. I think she kind of likes to lord it over me."

Elise merely hummed.

"Th… that's your answer?" Hayley asked.

"No." Elise moved from the desk to sit next to her on the bed and draped her arm around Hayley's shoulders.

"My answer is that you should explore this relationship. It sounds like she's passionate about something and that something is you. This woman is like no one you've ever met before, am I right?"

"You're right," Hayley said.

"So what's holding you back?"

What was holding her back? Hayley rolled her eyes. "The way she talks drives me insane and not in a good way. She is so cryptic sometimes and I think she's making fun of me, mocking me for being some naïve girl from the flat Midwest. It ticks me off."

"Ah, that makes sense, but you know what? You're smarter than any snarky, spoiled city girl." Elise turned to face Hayley and pushed her long, brown hair back off her friend's shoulders. "Look at you – you're a catch and you've spent the past four years doing nothing but working your pretty little ass off. Graduation is upon us. I think you ought to get to know this woman. If she gives you shit, you're smart enough to give it back to her. And if it doesn't work out, so what? At least start doing something more with your life than just working, girl. Seriously."

Hayley bowed her head and nodded. "Thanks, Elise. I appreciate that."

"Well, I mean it. All work and no play make Hayley a dull girl. If you've found someone you like, why not see where it goes? Have you gone on any dates with her yet?"

"Two." Hayley grimaced. "They weren't good, but I still can't get her out of my mind." Then again, she hadn't been able to get Veronica out of her mind since the storage room incident, something she wasn't about to reveal to Elise.

"Then you need to find a way to either make it work or forget about her. Which is it going to be?"

Hayley compressed her lips and pondered the question. Which, indeed.

Chapter 6

"I'M KIND OF SURPRISED you asked me out."
Veronica nudged Hayley with her shoulder and gave her
a sly smile. "I thought you were done with me."

"Oh, that I was." Hayley knew she sounded wry, but
she hoped Veronica would take it as a joke. Something
uncoiled within her – that need to always strive for
something, she realized – and with its hold loosened, she
felt more able to relax in Veronica's presence. It was
very different than when she was at school and felt the
pressure to accomplish things constantly.

"You're hilarious. So." Veronica held her hands
clasped before her as they walked. "To what do I owe
this pleasure? And you should know it is a pleasure to
have a pretty girl next to me on this warm, perfect spring
day."

Yes, Hayley realized that, and it was a pleasure for
her to be walking with a gorgeous woman who was
interested in her as more than a potential fling. That and
who seemed to go much deeper than initial appearances
suggested. "Actually, I did the digging you

recommended and you were right. It was well worth my time."

"Oh, I recommended you do that?" Veronica pressed her hands to her chest and gave Hayley a flirtatious batting of her eyelashes. Damn, that was cuter than she wanted to admit, Hayley realized. "What did you find out about me?"

Hayley tried to relax. They had exchanged a few texts over the past week, but Hayley had made it clear she needed time to deal with school before they could see each other again. Now finals were over and she had nailed a job. It wasn't the one she hoped for, but she was still happy with it. It was a step in the right direction, anyway, a legitimate journalism job to have on her resume.

She almost hated quitting the coffee shop, because it had become nice to see Veronica there every day. Today was officially her last day there and she had asked Veronica to meet her at the end of her shift to celebrate. Somehow they ended up walking around the Lincoln Memorial Reflecting Pool.

"Well, I think you can guess without me telling you,"

Hayley said. "Your life is pretty much all over any and all media that has ever existed."

Veronica laughed. "Playing coy, I see. I must be a bad influence. But I would prefer it if you enlightened me, Hayley. Please."

Hayley shook her head, the gentle breeze picking up her hair and lifting it off her face. For a moment, she turned to the wind, closed, her eyes, and savored it. Four years of school and work, and she could finally enjoy her life now that the crunch was over. Proving herself in her new job wouldn't be as hard as the constant need to study, perform, and test well. She slowly opened her eyes and looked at Veronica.

"Fine. I know you're forty-years-old and you modeled pretty much big-time until 2015. You've actually built your own fortune, despite being the daughter of a senator who has been in office since before I was born. So my assessment of you as a spoiled brat is sort of correct, but not perfectly right."

"Ouch. Spoiled brat. But not entirely, eh? Why do you say that?" The way Veronica tilted her head reminded Hayley of a fox. An adorable, but sly creature that seemed to be assessing her, determining just how much she knew. But Hayley wasn't ready to give it all up just yet. She could play Veronica's game just as well, now that she had more information on her.

"Because." It wasn't often that Hayley flounced, but she attempted it now and with what she thought was a good result. She heard Veronica laugh and then catch up to her.

"You, my dear, are learning." Veronica squinted at her and touched the tip of her index finger to Hayley's nose. "Lesson one is not to tell someone everything you know. Keep some secrets, some mystery, even. D.C.'s currency is intelligence, after all."

It felt like a victory, but it also felt like Veronica was still laughing at her. At least a little bit. "You'd think I would have remembered that after bingeing on TV shows about living here." It was strange how much lighter Hayley felt with the knowledge she had about Veronica. Sure, she still had questions about Veronica, but she knew far more than she had on their first date.

"Right? Too bad they aren't true to real life. Except maybe *House of Cards*. That one is pretty damn accurate. Trust me. Things are cut throat on Capitol Hill."

Now it was Hayley's turn to laugh. She didn't feel like the playing field was leveled between them just yet, but she did feel as though she had gained some ground. For once, hanging out together was turning out to be fun. Not just a strange game of cat and mouse, or some kind of spontaneous sex thing. Though she wouldn't have minded some spontaneous sex. With the pressure of finals and work off until after graduation, she felt like she had tension to release.

"Okay, I have to admit, there's one question I've been dying to ask you," Hayley finally said.

"Just one?"

"Well, several." Hayley hated to put it out there, but lying wasn't her strong suit. So she stuck with the most pressing question. "Why me? Why that night at the gala and why are you dating me?"

To her surprise, a blush rose to Veronica's cheeks. It wasn't a dramatic one, but it was still noticeable. "I think I told you I had a crush on you ever since you started working at the coffee shop. I'm not sure what it was about you. It wasn't just the way you looked, but how you smiled and spoke. I wanted to know the girl behind the 'Can I help you?' smile."

"I feel a little bad that I didn't really pay as much attention to you. I mean, I recognized you when you walked in, of course, but I hate to say I didn't really keep track of customers all that well, except..." Hayley paused and looked down at the sidewalk. "Except after the gala. I mean, you were memorable before that, but unforgettable after."

"Unforgettable?" Veronica did that head-tilt again and Hayley's heart melted. It didn't matter anymore how they first noticed each other. They were here together now. "I like that." Veronica linked her arm with Hayley's as they strolled alongside the reflecting pool.

For a few moments, they walked in silence and Hayley enjoyed it. It was one of those rare moments when the silence was not filled with work of some kind, but a pleasant activity. How often did she walk simply for pleasure these days? Rarely, if ever. Even friends like Elise only caught her in passing between classes or school and work.

"You know, I like you a lot." Veronica finally spoke again.

"Yeah, I definitely know that."

"No. I mean…" They stopped and Veronica turned to face her. "I don't just like you in a you're-a-cute-coed-fling way. I like you as a person. Yeah, the first thing I saw was that gorgeous brown hair, your sweet face, and all. But it's your personality that won me. You should know I've had years of practice at judging people and really looking at who they are beneath everything, and you are a special woman."

Hayley realized if she was prone to blushing, she would be doing it right now. Instead, though, something else happened to her body. Her heartbeat quickened and she felt a strange flicker in her belly. Butterflies?

"Then again, I've always had a thing for earnest Midwestern girls with brown eyes."

Now Hayley knew she felt something physical. Her breath caught and she stared at Veronica, not sure where else to look. They couldn't kiss right here, could they? In that moment, she certainly wanted to. What better place to share this moment than here at one of the most culturally profound places in their nation's capital?

Veronica leaned toward her and Hayley thought for a moment the kiss would happen. And then Veronica took a step back and her gaze dipped to the ground. "There's only one problem with me taking something like this public."

"Your father," Hayley acknowledged.

"You did do your homework. Good girl." A sigh lifted those slender shoulders and Veronica shook her head. "So you found out my dirty, dirty secret. My father is not just a senator, but probably the most conservative of the lot. If there's a bill that stands in the way of personal freedom or expression, he's probably behind it. There are plenty of well-meaning conservatives on the political spectrum. I don't diss them as a whole, but my father? He's on the extreme end. When I was in high school, he gave me plenty of reminders that if my sexuality messed up his career, he'd be through with me as a daughter."

Hayley didn't know what to say to that. She had grown up pretty happy with her family. Sure, her parents worked hard and weren't always there for her or her sister. Hayley had to pick up some of the slack more often than not, while her parents labored to make ends meet. But even without money, there had been unconditional love all around.

"Not that I don't love my father," Veronica assured her. "I'm sure you're thinking I must hate him. I don't. I disagree with him and I wish he would put love before his so-called family values, but I don't hate him."

"Okay, so I know you're already forty years old and have already done so much in your life, but I've got what might seem like an odd question."

"Go for it."

"Well, where do you see yourself in life?" Hayley glided her foot along the pavement and listened to the sound the sole of her shoe made against it. "I mean, I know you're at an age where you've pretty much paid your dues as far as your career, but is this where you plan to stay – stuck in a city where you can't ever live your life out in the open for fear of your father's reaction or what his constituents might think or how his enemies might use it against him?"

When Veronica let out a long, hearty laugh, Hayley

knew she'd said something completely off the mark.

"Now that I know my question is hilarious, why don't you enlighten me as to the reason it's so funny."

"I'm sorry." Veronica pressed her hand to her chest and gave her the dazzling grin that seemed to be her trademark expression. "You think I've lived my life behind closed doors because of my father? I haven't. And if you look at any number of politicians' children, you will find that the majority of them don't – pardon my language – give a flying fuck about their parents' careers."

Once again, Hayley was intrigued by this woman. Veronica seemed to be one thing but then surprised her by revealing herself as another. It was a game, Hayley realized, a game Veronica couldn't help but play. She'd grown up in the shark tank of D.C. and had to learn to swim with the big fish or else. Hayley was no longer frustrated by Veronica's verbal parrying. She was impressed that this beautiful woman was so cool and savvy underneath her perfect exterior.

"What I do care about is how I look to others," Veronica confessed. "The more of a rock-solid reputation I build, the less anyone will care when I finally come out as a lesbian. So I've spent my life building my own career and supporting a number of charities. Of course, they're all charities that fight what my father stands against. I've contributed a great deal of money to LGBT causes and lobbyists. If my father ever saw my tax returns, he'd be livid. But, again, I don't care. I feel that as long as I quietly and discreetly do what I can for the good of others, I'm being true to myself. The only thing missing is…"

At that, Veronica stopped, reached out, and took Hayley's hand. They both dropped their gazes and Hayley took a moment to consider how different they looked – Veronica tanned from her tennis outings, but delicate despite the physical activity. Hayley's own hand was pale from all the time she spent either at school or work, also delicate, but she knew how to do things Veronica could never imagine, such as operate farm equipment.

"I don't think I can stop this time," Veronica whispered. "I don't care that we're out here. Let the paparazzi take pictures all they want."

Hayley leaned in, sure she would never be able to catch her breath again once Veronica's lips touched hers. Their first kiss at the gala had been spontaneous and ravenously hungry. This one was sweet, with only the slightest tilting of their heads before they parted.

"Wow," Hayley said.

"I second that."

They both glanced around the pool, but Hayley didn't hear the click of cameras or any scandalized whispers. In fact, no one was near them. The only walkers were all the way across the pool, on the opposite corner. *Well, good.*

"So, where does that leave us right now?" Hayley asked.

"That's a good question." Veronica took her hand and this time didn't let it go. It felt nice to stroll hand-in-hand with someone for once, so Hayley went with it. Warmth flooded her body. So this was how it felt to be with someone she liked. "Do you have any more finals this week?"

"They're all done. My last one was Friday. I'm pretty sure I did well."

"And what about job interviews? How are those going?"

This was where Hayley hesitated. She lingered too long, she realized, because she felt Veronica give her hand a tug.

"Hayley?"

"Sorry. I…" Hayley rubbed the back of her neck and winced. Was she developing a physical affectation now, after all this time? "I got a job."

"Awesome! Did you get the *Washington Post*?"

The expectant way Veronica looked at her almost made her cringe. She had yet to break the news to anyone else, the awful news that she hadn't managed to bag her dream job. But Hayley shook her head and said, "Not exactly. I interviewed, but they didn't hire me."

"Oh, fuck them." Veronica looked fiercer than Hayley had ever seen her. "Do you want me to put in a call? I'm sure I can get you in there. They love me. I mean, I'm no Deep Throat, but I've passed on my share of information to the reporters there. And you did not hear that from me."

"Of course not." It was a strange sort of oversharing,

but Hayley appreciated it. "Actually, I'm happy with the job I got. It's at the *Feminist Flag* with a friend of mine from college. We used to run a column together in the college newspaper – a black/white perspective – and the *Flag* wants us to do it with them, too."

Veronica clapped her hands together and grinned. "I love it. My father would shit himself if he knew I was dating you. Though that's the exact reason why I keep my relationships private. I'm not out to get the old man or anything like that. I just want to find love, like everybody else in this world. Still…" She spun with glee and Hayley took a step back.

"So you're forty going on fourteen, I see."

"Har har, you're so funny. But get used to it. I tend to show my enthusiasm when I can. In a city where we get ahead by hiding our true feelings, it's nice to let loose every so often. We could both learn a thing or two about letting go. Am I right?"

Hayley couldn't remember the last time she had "let loose." The gala was an exception to her own stifling personal rules. She reached out and took Veronica's hand.

"Do you think you could help me do that?"

Chapter 7

GRADUATION DAY WAS EVERYTHING Hayley dreamed and more. Other than the fact that her parents couldn't be there, of course. But May was a crucial time on the farm. Heck, every day was crucial for farmers, even in the winter. Hayley more than understood.

Besides, she had two unexpected supporters who had used the tickets she had to offer. Her younger sister, Amber, sat in the audience grinning from ear to ear, a bunch of flowers clutched in her hands. And Veronica was only one row behind her, also holding a bouquet of flowers.

Hayley couldn't suppress her own grin as she crossed the stage to accept her diploma as one of the summa cum laude graduates of her class. Granted, it was a liberal arts degree with a minor in journalism, but she was the first person in her family to attend and graduate from college. This was not just a personal triumph. It meant something more than a good job and high-paying future.

When she sat back down next to Elise, she nudged

her and whispered, "Guess who's here."

"Who?" Elise looked stunning as usual and Hayley felt giddy despite not getting the job at the *Washington Post*. Having Elise as both a friend and competitor at school had kept her on her toes and forced her to work harder, to hone her craft. They would be a powerful pairing at the *Feminist Flag* and Hayley looked forward to a future with a fantastic co-worker and...

"Veronica." Hayley pointed her out as subtly as she could.

"Wow," Elise said under her breath. "She's a looker. Too bad I don't play for the other team. So, are you two an official thing at this point or what?"

As Hayley peeked at her diploma, she shrugged. "Not quite yet, but we're getting there. No commitment at this time, but I thought about what you said and realized dating someone who's my opposite would be good for me. The more I talk to her, though, the more I realize we're pretty similar at heart."

"Intriguing. You're going to have to keep me informed." Elise smiled and then hugged Hayley. "I'm glad you're finally doing something for you, Hay. I mean, I know working your ass off all these years has been for you, but there are other rewards to be reaped in life."

"I know. My focus has been entirely on academics and my professional future. I still feel the pressure to prove myself. We're new graduates, after all, but I think..." Hayley glanced over her shoulder at Veronica again and then back toward the front of the assembly. "I think opening myself up to romance is a good thing. I don't need to be so damn stoic all the time."

The final graduates crossed the stage and Elise elbowed her. "Then I guess this is where we don't hang on to our hats. Stoked for the future, Hay?"

Hayley reached for her cap and nodded. "Stoked."

As the Dean congratulated their class, Hayley and Elise both jumped to their feet and tossed their caps. Hayley scrambled to recover hers, though. She might not have been much for girly gestures, but she had a sentimental nature. There was no way she wanted to let go of this keepsake, this reminder of how hard she had worked to achieve everything in her life.

"I can't believe we did it!" Elise squealed, grasping

her by the shoulders and shaking her. "This is it! Our lives can begin!"

Hayley wanted to point out their lives began more than twenty years ago, but instead she smiled and nodded. "To the next phase," she said. Her gaze traveled to the crowd of attendees and she said, "I think it's time to mingle."

"Right. We have to let the people who love us be all proud and mushy." Elise tossed her long, dark hair over her shoulder and waved at someone Hayley couldn't see. "My brother's here! I have to go. See you later."

Hayley watched how Elise ran and flung herself into the arms of a tall, uniformed African-American man. She remembered Elise's brother was in the Army and had been deployed for a while. With a smile, Hayley watched how her friend laughed and cried simultaneously. It had to be hard to have someone you loved gone for so long, especially somewhere dangerous. Hayley couldn't relate, but she could understand Elise's joy at having him home on this special day.

"Hay-Hay," came a quiet voice and she turned to face her little sister.

"Amberston," Hayley answered, wrapping her arms around the petite brunette girl standing behind her. "It's so good to see you."

And it was. She missed her little sister something fierce. Maybe it had something to do with the fact that her parents had worked hard day after day, and ultimately Hayley had replaced any babysitter when it came to her sister. Even from a young age, Hayley had mothered Amber in some ways. She was there to teach her to read, to snuggle her at night when there was a thunderstorm, and to keep her feeling secure. It wasn't that her parents hadn't done all of that. It was just that owning a farm, especially a struggling one, was a twenty-four/seven job.

As it turned out, it was a job Amber loved. After graduating from high school, she took over all the business aspects of the farm from their parents and even lent a hand when it came to the manual labor.

"Thank you for these. How is everyone?" Hayley asked as she accepted the small, plastic-wrapped bouquet of flowers from her sister.

"Mom and Dad are working too hard, as usual, but

it's May so…" Amber shrugged as if to indicate that was to be expected. "Remember when Aunt Regina passed away in January? It turns out, she left everything to Mom."

"Well, that makes sense," Hayley said. "I mean, she didn't have a spouse or kids."

"Yeah. Well, it turns out what she had was an insanely valuable estate. We made some big changes with the money and finally hired help. Ron and Benito are awesome. They're from Mexico and, holy crap, they know their grapes. Dad thought we were crazy to try growing them, but guess what we started growing?"

Hayley rolled her eyes. "Grapes?"

"Yup and we'll have our first harvest this season. Not only that, but we're going to experiment with making wine. Isn't that something? Thanks to Ron and Ben, and Aunt Regina's estate, I think Mom has finally gotten to where she can have eight hours of sleep a night. It's nice to see her taking it easy."

Hayley's shoulders relaxed. Even though her parents were still young, she couldn't help but think they ought to start slowing down, at least a little. Her father seemed like he'd always been strong, sturdy, built for the life he chose. But her mother was a slight woman. Sure, she could haul hay with Hayley but, at some point, she would have to slow down. Right?

"What about you? Do you ever sleep?" Amber blinked up at her with wide, brown eyes, and Hayley stared back in disbelief.

Was she serious? When had Hayley ever...

"Ha!" Amber pointed at her. "I'm kidding. I know you don't sleep. You're always on overdrive. Hayley the turbo achiever."

"Very funny. I'll have you know I've taken it down a notch. Don't make me give you a noogie here in front of everyone."

"You wouldn't dare."

Hayley wouldn't, but it was fun to have her little sister next to her again. She gave her another hug as if to assure herself Amber was real. "So I haven't told Mom and Dad yet, but I got a job and an apartment, too. Both are mine as of tomorrow."

"Wow, you work fast." Amber furrowed her brow. "I thought maybe you'd come home for a visit after graduation."

The way Amber's expression fell made Hayley feel awful. "I didn't even think about it," she admitted, regret blossoming within her chest. She hadn't gone home for Aunt Regina's funeral, either, she reminded herself. Instead, Hayley had been so caught up in the energy of her senior year, and then finals and nailing a job, that she hadn't given a single thought to the idea of seeing her family.

"No, no, it's fine," Amber said hastily. "You've been busy and now you have a brand new, exciting life waiting for you. No one wants you to put that on pause. No one."

"Yeah, but my life isn't more important than my family. I'm sorry, I really just didn't think and that's inexcusable, considering we lost Auntie this year," Hayley answered. "Why don't I see if I can get away for the weekend of July Fourth? I bet if I prove myself, I can get some early unpaid vacation time. Besides, it's an online news site, so I can probably negotiate to work remotely for a few days."

"Online news site…" Once again, Amber's brows

knit together and she looked confused. "What about the *Washington Post*, Hay? Or any newspaper? Working in print was always your dream."

"Oh." Hayley looked down at the grass and dug into it with the toe of her shoe. Sure, she had compromised, but that was only a temporary solution. "I interviewed at a few newspapers but didn't get a job offer. The one I got is at an up-and-coming news site that really caters to the Millennial demographic. It's definitely not where I see myself staying, not by any means, but it's a chance to get some experience under my belt. Trust me, it'll look better on my resume than 'Barista'."

Amber still looked disappointed, even as she nodded. "But you always dreamed of writing for a newspaper and having millions read your work. What about something closer to home, like the *Omaha World Herald*? They've got some fantastic journalists and that would be a pretty sweet gig – writing for a newspaper just like you wanted, but living only a couple of hours away from Mom and Dad."

"This website will get me millions of readers. Readership goes up every day. And like I said, it's just my first job, totally meant to pad my resume. Don't worry. I'll be on the lookout for bigger and better things." Hayley turned Amber toward the crowd and said, "Do you see that beautiful woman there with the long straight hair?"

"Her?" Amber asked, pointing at Elise.

"Yes. She became one of my best friends here and she's a complete genius. Together we're taking our *Georgetown Voice* perspectives column to this new website. I don't want to toot my own horn or anything, but I think it's going to be awesome."

"She is pretty spectacular to look at. You have a crush on her, don't you?"

"What?" Hayley pulled away from Amber and glared at her. "No! I mean, Elise is gorgeous, but she's straight and pretty much guy-crazy. In fact, you'd love hanging out with her. My point is she's one of the smartest women I've ever met and I seriously think our column about intersectional feminism will help get the *Feminist Flag* in front of a whole new audience."

Amber choked back laughter and shook her head. "Dad would crap himself if he knew you were working for something with a name like that."

"Maybe a little. But he'd understand." Hayley wished she could talk to Amber all day long, but she knew she had another guest waiting to see her. She wasn't sure she wanted anyone in her family to meet Veronica just yet. It wasn't that there was a problem with her sexual orientation. Even her fairly conservative parents had accepted it with very little fuss. Questions, sure, but little fuss.

Veronica wasn't quite her girlfriend yet, though, and Hayley didn't know how she would introduce her.

Veronica, however, seemed unperturbed about the situation, because she approached and offered the flowers to Hayley. "Congratulations on your graduation, Hayley. Is this your sister?"

"Yeah." Hayley took the flowers and nodded to Amber. Now she would have to make an introduction. "This is Amber. Amber, this is my friend, Veronica."

Amber and Veronica shook hands and Hayley let out a quiet breath. No questions so far. Good. "Hey, I bet you two want a picture together. Why don't you let me take some? I'm sure your parents would love it,"

Veronica offered.

"That would be great, thank you." Amber dug into her tote bag and pulled out a camera. "I imagine you feel comfortable using this?"

"A Nikon 3DX? Absolutely." And to prove her words, Veronica took off the lens cap, turned on the power and held the camera to her face. "Okay, get together, show me some sisterly love, and say 'cheese'."

She took several pictures and then Amber checked the photos while Hayley watched. "Wow, you are good," Amber said, turning off the camera and putting it away. "Most people don't know how to use this kind, but I'm not surprised you can do it."

"I learned everything I could about my work. I like knowing things. Though I was kind of afraid to touch a Hasselblad. If I broke it, I'd be out almost thirty grand, and that was a scary thought." Veronica winked at Hayley and then looked at Amber again. "I'm sure you two have plans to celebrate, so why don't I leave you to them. Hayley, thank you so much for inviting me to your graduation. Give me a call and we'll get together sometime after you're settled into your new apartment, okay?"

"Okay," Hayley said a little uncertainly. That was it? Wasn't Veronica going to pull some kind of sly shenanigans on her in front of Amber?

But no. The blonde simply leaned in and kissed her on the cheek, then whispered in her ear, "Thank you for inviting me to this special day. I hope to see many more of them."

The gesture ignited that giddy feeling within Hayley and she had trouble watching Veronica leave. She should invite her out with the two of them. No, she should let her go and explain to Amber alone. No, she should…

"Don't worry," Amber called after Veronica, "she's all yours tonight if you want her."

Veronica turned, somehow walking backward gracefully across the grass, even though she was wearing heels. "Thank you, Amber. In that case, I'll be in touch in a few hours."

"Oh my gosh, Amber!" Hayley hissed as she turned back to her sister. "Why would you say something like that?"

"Well, she obviously digs you. Are you dating her?"

"Maybe." When Amber narrowed her eyes, Hayley mirrored her expression. "Fine, yes. I am."

"I'm not surprised. She's even more stunning in real life than she is in magazines."

Hayley knew her mouth wanted to fall open, but she fought the urge and simply glared at her sister. "You know who she is?"

"Of course I do. So why don't you tell me how you ended up dating Veronica Stone-McClusky."

Chapter 8

"HAPPY GRADUATION TO YOU, Happy Graduation to you, Happy Graduation dear Hayley, Happy Graduation to you."

Hayley covered her eyes with her hands as Veronica set the cupcake down in front of her with a flourish. It was the first time anyone had sung to her in public and she just knew people were probably looking their way. When she peeked between her fingers, she saw that a flame flickered on the candle in the center of the cupcake.

"That's not even a real song," she told Veronica while the blonde settled in the chair across from her.

"I know, but who cares? A special day calls for a special song."

Hayley dropped her hands to see Veronica looking at her expectantly.

"Go on. Blow it out and make a wish."

"That's for birthdays."

"And graduation days because I say so." Veronica nodded toward the cupcake. "Get to it, Hayley Becker, or I'll have to do it for you. And you might not want what I would wish for tonight. Then again…" Veronica reached across the table to trace her thumb over Hayley's wrist. "You might want it very much."

Indecision warred within Hayley. Part of her wanted to pull away from that seductive touch and another part of her wanted to tell her how much she wanted what Veronica wanted. All that tension demanding release had been building and building, and she didn't think she could hold it in anymore. But she smiled and said, "Fine, I'll make a wish for you."

As she said it, Hayley realized Veronica could take the sentence personally. Maybe she should, though, considering Hayley was wishing for her at this very moment. When she blew out the candle, the resulting smoke spiraled upward and then dissipated. Their dark, private corner of the restaurant seemed intimate enough, even though another couple was having dinner only a few feet away from them. The standing screens helped, Hayley supposed. It was certainly the fanciest restaurant she had ever been to, and she was glad Veronica had the foresight to text her ahead of time with a message to dress nicely.

"So, how was your visit with your sister?" Veronica asked, propping her chin on her hand. They weren't there for dinner – just dessert and champagne. Hayley was still full enough from her celebratory lunch with Amber.

"It was great. She's doing well, my parents are doing well, and mostly they just can't wait to see me again. It's past time for me to visit home, so I really need to plan something this summer."

"Hmm..." Veronica plucked the cooled candle from the center of the cupcake and licked the vanilla frosting off the end of it.

Hayley waited for an explanation and then asked, "Is that all you have to say?"

"Sort of. What about you – do you want to see your parents again?"

"Yeah, I do. I kind of hate living so far away from them, but this is where I need to be to make my mark. First I need to get moved into the apartment and start my new job. We'll see what kind of vacation time I have after that."

Veronica pouted and muttered, "All work and no play makes Hayley a very dull girl."

Hayley narrowed her eyes at Veronica. "That's exactly what one of my friends said about me. Were you two comparing notes or something?"

"Maybe. You're one of my favorite topics, you know."

"Don't get cute with me." Even though Hayley said it, she realized she didn't quite mean it. Even with a move and new job looming, she felt free. Maybe it was because of the finality that came with graduation or maybe it was Veronica herself. Whatever it was, Hayley didn't want to lose that feeling. She wanted to savor it through the night.

So she leaned across the table and kissed Veronica.

It was a hungrier kiss than she anticipated, but she tempered it by pulling back just a bit. This was not the time or the place to give in to her lust. Not just yet.

But it was a familiar kiss, too, similar to the one they exchanged the night of the gala. The night Veronica had surprised her and then...

They'd already had sex. Was there even a question

of when the right time was to do it again? Hayley didn't think so. Hayley had lost count of their dates and she realized if she didn't do something about her lust, she would go crazy.

"Do you want to get out of here?" Veronica asked as Hayley sat back. Her eyes were glittering and her cheeks flushed. Even in the dim light, Hayley could see all the signs. Veronica wanted her as much as Hayley wanted Veronica.

Rather than give in to the usual "Too fast, too emotional, irrelevant to getting ahead, focus on what matters" voice in her head – the one that had governed her since the latter end of high school – Hayley nodded. They were adults and they didn't need to live by arbitrary rules about dating. They just needed to follow their hearts.

The cupcake remained uneaten on the table and that didn't matter one bit to Hayley because she was getting her wish.

Veronica directed her driver to bring them to her townhouse and Hayley silently acquiesced. Her dorm full of packed moving boxes was in no shape for a visitor, her twin-size bed no place for sex. *Right, I still need to buy a bed...*

And then she stifled the pragmatic little voice again, because Veronica's hands were in her hair, lips on hers, and they were caught up in a steamy embrace that left Hayley breathless. She was momentarily grateful for the tinted window that closed off the front seat from the back of the car. And as Veronica trailed her lips down along her neck, Hayley was grateful for having a driver, too. How would they have lasted if they had to walk or take a taxi to Veronica's place?

She didn't even wonder after that because she was lying across the plush seat with Veronica atop her. Those hands, so strong from weekends playing tennis, grasped her wrists tightly. Veronica's lips crushed down over hers and Hayley moaned against her mouth. They could do it here and now in the car and the driver wouldn't notice.

Veronica must have noticed when they stopped, though, because she sat up and pulled Hayley with her. "Come on," she whispered huskily. "We're there and I can't wait."

They got out of the car and Hayley was only vaguely aware of the cool night air on her heated skin. Veronica unlocked the front door quickly, not even fumbling in her excitement. If it had been Hayley, she probably would have dropped her keys more than once. But Veronica opened the door, tugged her inside, and then shut and locked the door behind them. The keys clattered to the surface of a table just inside the door and then Veronica's arms were around her.

Even though Hayley had never been in Veronica's townhouse before, she didn't pay any attention to the exterior or the interior. As soon as they embraced, their bodies seemed locked together. It was a connection forged by desire and neither one of them was eager to break it.

Hayley didn't know if they'd end up in the bedroom. She didn't care, either. All the feelings and wants she normally kept repressed finally bubbled to the surface, demanding release. Nothing mattered but this beautiful woman and the undeniable heat between them.

Veronica pressed her against a wall on the opposite side of the living room from the front door and her hands clutched at Hayley's waist, before pushing up to cup her breasts. Hayley had her arms tight around Veronica's neck as they kissed, mouths slanted over one another's, a perfect fit.

"It's your day," Veronica said against Hayley's lips, "so allow me."

And then she was sinking to her knees before Hayley. This gorgeous, wealthy, powerful woman on her knees in front of a farmer's daughter yet again. It was wild, as far as Hayley was concerned, and she sank back against the wall with her legs spread as Veronica's head went up under the short skirt of her dress.

Those delicate hands with their slender fingers drifted up along Hayley's torso again, locking over her breasts as Veronica nuzzled her way between Hayley's thighs. She had some serious talent with her tongue, Hayley thought hazily, because she somehow managed to get into her panties without using her hands.

"Oh my god," Hayley breathed as Veronica's tongue drew a long, hard path along her slit. She was glad she had taken the time to get a pre-graduation wax from head to toe. It had been the one thing she splurged on during her four years of college – getting waxed at the spa, so she wouldn't have to waste time shaving every week.

Veronica certainly seemed to appreciate it, because she hummed with approval as her tongue delved between Hayley's lower lips. For a brief, giddy moment, Hayley thought of the scene in *Young Frankenstein* when the doctor mentioned making the "yummy sound," and she giggled.

Damn it! She had never giggled during sex before. What was wrong with her?

It didn't matter, though, because Veronica's next maneuver took her breath away. The deeper Veronica went in tasting her, the more Hayley sagged against the wall and onto her searching tongue. It was like something out of a movie, something sensual and passionate. She didn't want it to end.

No. She wanted to orgasm *now*.

But… she wanted more… right?

Which was it?

Hayley realized that it didn't matter what her racing mind thought… or thought it thought because her body had already taken over. And it was dragging her, quite suddenly, over the edge. She closed her eyes and leaned her head back. She felt her mouth open and her hands grasping behind her, bracing her against the wall.

This was it. There was no stopping the orgasm. Her body's reaction went into complete overdrive, shaking uncontrollably. She didn't know if she would be able to stay standing. The only thing that made her feel even the least bit secure was the way Veronica continued to hold her upright, hands pushing up hard against her breasts, mouth fastened against her pussy tightly.

And for the first time in her life, Hayley gave herself permission to lose complete control of her mind and body. Her own yells sounded loud in her ears, but she didn't care, didn't try to stop it or rein it in. She just let go of every barrier she had put up since her adolescence. Let go and rode the wave of bliss that carried her back down against Veronica's strong, sure body.

As Hayley felt herself falling, Veronica was there to catch her. Hayley opened her eyes and belatedly realized Veronica was standing, arms around her.

"This is why you need to learn to play," Veronica

whispered, before kissing her lightly. "Because it's so damn fun when you give in."

Hayley didn't have the strength to respond, let alone move, but she didn't have to. Veronica laid her down on the sofa. The fact that they were in the living room registered in Hayley's mind after a heartbeat, but that was all.

Because now Veronica was stretched out atop her, arm between their bodies and her fingers...

"Oh god!" Hayley arched into that touch, those fingers thrusting in and out of the slickness of her dewy valley. The sights, sounds, tastes, smells, and feelings were beyond intimate. Veronica had none of the hesitation of Hayley's partners from high school or early in college. Another giddy thought entered her mind: *She sure knows her way around a vagina.*

This time, though, she didn't giggle. She just sighed and clutched at Veronica's shoulders, lost in the rapture and freedom of the moment. Sex should be fun. It was okay to have silly thoughts and to laugh and cry and...

Her body arched up against Veronica's, her legs spread wider, and then she felt the overwhelming ecstasy again. It was something she had to catch and keep for herself.

"Look at me," Veronica whispered. "I want to watch you come."

No one had ever said that to her before and Hayley fought to keep her eyes open, to keep her gaze locked on Veronica's. The intensity of the orgasm that overtook her body made it impossible for Hayley to maintain her focus perfectly, but the smile on Veronica's face told her she didn't care. It had been enough that Hayley held on as long as she did, looked at her as commanded until her control shattered into a million tingling pieces.

With a deep breath, Hayley relaxed into the sofa, her tension gone. For now. It was something she knew would return, something she would return to Veronica to alleviate again. No other woman would do. She blinked her way back to consciousness and placed her hands on either side of Veronica's face.

"When do I get to return the favor?" she asked. After all, Veronica had gotten to know her quite intimately and Hayley had given her nothing more than a few kisses. Even through the ecstatic haze, Hayley knew she wanted to get to know Veronica. She needed to hold her, kiss her, touch her, taste her, and more.

"You can do it whenever you want to." Veronica tilted her head and smiled down at her. "But I have a feeling you still need to recover, at least a little bit. Why don't we go to bed?"

Hayley felt a cool trail along her cheek. A tear. She blinked any others away before they could fall. Veronica lifted her hand to Hayley's face and wiped her thumb along the cool, wet path.

"You're crying a little. Are you okay?"

"Sorry. I'm just feeling so much." Hayley didn't know what else to say without babbling, so she clamped her lips together against the words that clamored against them. *That was amazing. I think I love you. I can't love you yet, but I think I do. Why did I wait so long? What do you do to me? Again, again, again.*

"Don't be sorry. I think it's beautiful," Veronica whispered. "You're beautiful, Hayley. Come on. Let me put you to bed. I've been wanting to get you in here for a while now."

Somehow, Hayley found herself on her feet, warm

and secure in the circle of Veronica's arms. Each step dissipated the erotic fog that clouded her mind and when they reached the bedroom, she turned and pressed a lingering kiss on Veronica's lips.

They were full, plush lips with a hint of saltiness on them – the taste of Hayley herself. Hayley never wanted to stop kissing. "You," she muttered. I want to do the same things to you."

"And I want to tuck you into my bed and never let you leave it." Veronica looked earnest for once.

"That sounds good to me." Hayley wrapped her arms around the blonde and kissed her as hard as she could. Now that her senses were returning, she wanted to steal Veronica's from her. So she tumbled with her into the bed and worked on doing just that.

Chapter 9

SUNLIGHT, BRILLIANT AND GOLDEN. It filtered into the bedroom through the blinds, along with the sound of birdsong. Hayley never saw one or heard the other in her dorm room, and she rolled over to look for the source.

Right, this wasn't her dorm room. It was Veronica's spacious bedroom in her townhouse. The sheets smelled like Veronica and Hayley almost wanted to roll over and hug the other pillow to her.

Instead, though, Hayley sat up and looked around, while smacking her lips lightly. It was the first time she had ever slept over someone else's house, with the exception of the standard teenage sleepover involving chick flicks, popcorn, and painting each other's toenails.

Those sleepovers certainly hadn't involved sex, let alone the insane amount of sex she and Veronica had the night before. Hayley tried to remember everything they had done together. Even after making Veronica orgasm twice, she hadn't wanted to stop. No, Hayley wanted to continue, so they did until they were both exhausted.

All that control Hayley prided herself on had gone

right out the window and she gladly let it. Why was that? She rose from the bed, sheets clutched to her naked body. The next question she wondered about was where the hell her clothes had gone. They were nowhere to be seen and she finally gave up searching the bedroom. After a trip to the bathroom, she wandered into the kitchen, still swathed in those crisp, Veronica-scented sheets.

There was Veronica, at the stove, flipping a pancake.

"You're joking," Hayley said. "Pancakes, really? Isn't that a little cliché?"

"Batter up!" Veronica slid the pancake on a plate and set it on the small white table in the breakfast nook. "Are you telling me this isn't your thing?"

"I've just never…" Hayley glanced around the townhouse. "Wow, this place is really nice. I didn't get a good look last night, but you have amazing taste."

"Thanks. It was the first major thing I bought with my own hard-earned money. I've been here for years. I love it. Sometimes I think I could use a change of scenery, but maybe that's because I'm here alone most of the time. Being alone gets boring fast." Veronica poured more batter into the skillet and then went to the refrigerator. "Can I get you some orange juice, coffee, or tea?"

"I'll drink anything. I'm not picky." Hayley hesitated before she sank into the chair at the table.

"Why don't I make mimosas, then? But I suppose clothing might be a must." Now that usual playful smirk was back on Veronica's face.

Hayley averted her gaze to the pancake waiting for her. "Yeah, that might be helpful."

"I like you like this, though." Veronica circled the table, stood behind Hayley, bent over, and wrapped her arms around her. "It's adorable. How often do you just wander around in a sheet?"

"Never." She was always one of the first girls to the showers, robed, caddy and towel in hand, ready to tackle the day.

"Then enjoy it. After today, you're a working girl." Veronica stepped away and chuckled to herself. "I mean, not a working girl, you know, but as in you're a young lady with a job. Plus with your move today, you need a good breakfast."

"Oh, crap!" Hayley looked at the clock on the microwave and half-rose from the chair. "Yeah, I have to get my stuff out of the dorm like... now!"

"No worries." The other woman walked over to Hayley, placed her hands on her shoulders, and gently urged her to sit down. "Just eat breakfast, get a shower, and I'll take care of the rest."

Even though Hayley expected her stomach to tie up in nervous knots over not adhering to the schedule she'd set for herself for moving day, it didn't. She wolfed down the pancake and then the second one Veronica slid onto her plate. When she was full, she excused herself to shower.

In the bathroom, she took a moment to admire the shiny tiling on the walls and decorative flooring. The shower was big, with a sliding door and generous shelves. Hayley used Veronica's high-end brand shampoo and conditioner, lathered up with the scented body wash, and rinsed.

When she opened the shower door, her dress was on a hanger on the inside of the bathroom door and her underthings were folded neatly on top of a small, low table. By the time Hayley emerged from the bathroom, she almost didn't want to leave the luxurious townhome. It was a heck of a lot bigger than her dorm room and far nicer than the apartment she had secured. Even though Hayley wasn't one to yearn for nice things, she couldn't help but linger.

But Veronica was at the door, dressed, purse dangling from her wrist, and phone in hand. "There, isn't that better?" she asked.

"Much," Hayley admitted.

"You didn't have a lot of stuff to move, so my guys already have it at your apartment. They're unloading now. We just need to tell them where to put it."

"Wha? Really?" Hayley blinked and shook her head. "I'm sorry, could you repeat that."

"After your graduation ceremony, I put some movers on the job for today. I hope you don't mind. I really wanted you to take some of the burdens off your shoulders if I could. It's my graduation gift to you." Uncertainty creased Veronica's brow for a moment before smoothing out. "Is that okay with you or did I just overstep?"

Hayley wasn't sure how to feel. She certainly didn't need to be rescued or cared for by a too-wealthy political princess. But she had to admit it felt nice – very nice – to be taken care of by someone else for a change. This would take some getting used to.

Veronica still looked worried. "I'm sorry if I overstepped by boundaries, but as you can see I have a habit of doing that with you."

"Yeah. No. I mean…" Hayley shook her head again and swept her bangs out of her eyes. "Actually, I appreciate that. Thanks. That's a wonderful gift, right up my alley."

"I figured this would free up the rest of your day for furniture shopping and don't you have to check in at the office as well?"

That was true. She and Elise had a late meeting with their new boss to establish their schedule and discuss their first assignment.

"Shall we be on our way?" Veronica opened the door for Hayley and then followed her outside to her waiting car. "I know you think I'm a privileged brat, but privilege has its perks."

"I guess so." Hayley slid into the car and settled back in the seat. When Veronica sat down, Hayley turned to her and said, "You know, I never expected my life to include any of this."

"Any of what?" The way Veronica blinked told Hayley she really didn't understand her meaning, so Hayley gestured at the plush interior of the vehicle.

"Rides in snazzy cars with chauffeurs, breakfast in a beautiful multi-million dollar townhouse with a former model and politician's daughter. I didn't come to D.C. to rub elbows with the rich and powerful. I came here to tell the world the truth through the news, to keep them informed of things they should know. I came here to work hard in pursuit of that truth because people deserve to know what's going on around them."

A long silence passed between them and Hayley wondered if maybe she'd said something wrong. Then Veronica leaned over and kissed her. "This is why I'm falling in love with you," she said. "You're passionate about something important. You have integrity and ethics, and you are everything this city lacks. We need more people like you here."

It was the sweetest thing Veronica had said to her, and Hayley scooted over so they were pressed against each other and she could rest her head on Veronica's shoulder. Once again, she was struck by how nice it felt to just be together, with a person she liked as more than a friend.

They arrived at her new apartment where a moving van sat open and three men were carrying Hayley's boxes inside. It wasn't the best side of town, but it wasn't the worst, either. Hayley was grateful she could afford an apartment in one of the quieter areas of D.C., not far from work or the various coffee shops and bakeries where she might want to get her caffeine and sweets fix.

"How did they get into my apartment?" she asked Veronica.

"I called the landlord and asked for access. It wasn't difficult. You're in good hands with me. And this place..." Veronica nodded at it. "This is the perfect neighborhood for you. Kind of hipsterish, but that's why I like it."

They emerged from the car and Hayley walked into

the building. Her apartment door stood open and some of the boxes were already placed in there. There wasn't much, but it was nice to have someone else doing the work. The boxes were well-labeled, too, and the movers seemed to have heeded those labels. Anything marked "kitchen" was in the kitchen, "bedroom" was in the bedroom... and it seemed everything was under control.

So Hayley stood back and watched with a shake of her head. "Oh crap, what about my laptop and stuff?" she asked Veronica.

"No worries. They packed it. I had them pack everything in your desk, dresser, and closet. No stone unturned. I know that might feel kind of icky, but trust me. These guys are good." Veronica looked at her phone and said, "We can pick up the furniture you need and have it delivered, too. I know you've saved up, so you should buy something you really want. The bed needs to be first, though."

"So I can sleep tonight?" Hayley asked.

"Sure, that too." Veronica winked at her and tucked her phone away.

It was strange to think that buying a new bed would

mean more than using it for sleep now and that knowledge sent an unfamiliar thrill through Hayley. "I have one in mind," she said. "Here." She pulled out her own cell phone and showed Veronica the store where she had found the set she liked. "I mean, I'd love to buy the whole set, but I thought I'd just get the bed because I need that more than anything."

"Nonsense." Veronica pulled out her phone again and dialed a number. "Hi there Eddie, it's Veronica McClusky. How are you? Mmhm. And Teri and the kids? Fabulous. I'm glad to hear it."

Hayley grinned as she listened to the one-sided conversation. What the heck was Veronica up to now?

"So you have this gorgeous bedroom set on the store website," Veronica said, "and I have a friend who wants it today. We need delivery immediately. Can you work that out for me? Of course you can, because you're a doll."

When Veronica finished giving Hayley's new address, she ended the call and smiled at her. "Does that work for you?"

"Uh, yeah." Hayley used both hands to gather her

hair back behind her shoulders. "I mean, yeah, it does. That's nuts. But am I just going to hand cash to the delivery driver or something?"

"No, we'll swing by the store right now and you can pay for the set. And then while we're there, you can see if there's anything else you want. I know a dining room set could wait, but I'm sure you need at least some basic pots, pans, and dishes."

"I have that kind of stuff." Hayley thought of her mismatched hand-me-down plates and cooking utensils. "I'll replace all of it one of these days, but it would be nice to look and see if there's anything I like."

"Great. Let's go."

And just like that, everything fell into place. It was a strange new world for Hayley. Being with Veronica opened all kinds of doors, she realized. She noticed when Veronica used her father's name and when she used her mother's name. More often than not, she used her mother's name – Stone – and was granted anything she wished. Her father's name, McClusky, seemed to be the name she used when she wanted something done immediately. Either way, it was a heady experience to have someone wielding that kind of power on her behalf.

Another thing Hayley noticed was Veronica was always charming and polite. She never behaved as though she was entitled to first class service, never demanded it. She would start a conversation, be personable and sweet, and usually get what she wanted, even without the name-dropping.

As her driver brought them to Hayley's work meeting, Hayley just looked at her.

Veronica blinked at her and asked, "What is it?"

"I just..." Hayley fell silent and smoothed her dress over her knees. She could have changed, but the dress was appropriate enough for the work environment. Plus, Veronica must have washed and pressed it, because it smelled fresh and had no wrinkles.

"What is it?" Veronica asked again.

"I feel kind of bad," Hayley admitted, "like I misjudged you when we first met."

"Oh, honey. Everyone does that."

Hayley laced her fingers around her knee and said, "Maybe, but I should be better than that, considering my blathering about the pursuit of truth earlier. When we went on our first and second dates, I thought you were a spoiled brat, but you're actually a really nice person. You don't just snap your fingers and expect things, and when you do get things, you always say thank you. You talk to people like you really know them and care about them."

"I do care." Veronica glanced at the window that separated them from the driver and said, "Take Armand, for instance. He's a refugee from Haiti. When he got here five years ago, I helped guide him through the immigration process. Once he was settled, we were able to also get his wife and children over here. Now, I could have hired a driver anywhere, right?"

Hayley nodded.

"But D.C. is full of highly-skilled workers and college graduates. They don't want to work as drivers. They want to pursue their ambitions. After years of living in Haiti, all Armand wanted was a place where his family could be safe, where his kids could get a good education. He wanted a job no one else did, and I wanted to make a difference. What we've done in getting him and his family citizenship will resonate for generations.

His son and daughter will have opportunities they might not have gotten otherwise, and so will their kids and their kids' kids. That's not about me. That's bigger than me."

Something shimmered in Veronica's eyes and she turned away, wiping at the tears with her fingers.

Hayley held her breath and just watched this woman who was so gorgeous, so together, and so rich. She had everything.

Including an amazing heart.

Hayley reached out and curled her hand around Veronica's. How fortunate she was, she knew, to be in that heart too.

Chapter 10

"YOU WANT TO WRITE an article on what?" Jill repeated.

Hayley swallowed and glanced down at her notes. Why did her new boss sound so snide?

It was Monday morning, the first full week of her job. She had spent a long, wonderful weekend with Veronica, who insisted on helping her settle into the new apartment. The first work meeting after graduation had gone well, she thought. Jill, her editor-in-chief, told her and Elise to pull all their *Georgetown Voice* columns and pitch the ones they thought could be revamped for fresh publication. At the time, Jill seemed enthusiastic about the perspectives angle.

"It's something different, something we haven't done, but you've received acclaim for at Georgetown. Now it's time for you to up your game," she'd told Hayley and Elise in their first meeting. "I want you to pick the columns you believe can be reworked for our audience and approach them in a new way."

That sounded like a great way for them to hit the

ground running and Hayley was excited. But over the weekend another idea had come to mind, an additional article she wanted to pitch. After her pitch, though, it was clear Jill didn't like it. Even now, the brunette's brow was knit and there was a sneer marring her angular face. The disgust radiating from her was palpable and Hayley had to force herself to continue sitting upright, to not give in to the urge to cringe.

"You want to write some touchy-feely drivel about the children of politicians who work against their parents' ideals, who do good in the world for women, children, and others." The way Jill threw her idea back at her was like a slap in the face.

Hayley fought to keep her voice steady as she said, "No, I want to point out how many politicians' children are enabling progress, rather than hindering it. You have to admit there are plenty of scandalous stories about kids who drink, gamble, and get in crazy accidents, but what if we get into the ones who stand up to their uber-conservative fathers, you know? I really want to focus on daughters here, not the sons boozing and carousing around wildly. They get enough press. Let's talk about how these women are making a difference."

"Becker, unless it's a pertinent expose that encourages our readers to take action, I have no interest in it. Who cares about do-gooder politicians' kids? All of them are useless, over-privileged brats. We're not here to give people a warm, happy, fluffy rah-rah feeling. Our mission is to inform them of the gross inequalities between men and women, between white and every other race. Not to celebrate a few politicians' kids who happen to donate money to a good cause every so often."

Hayley and Elise exchanged glances. Hayley could tell by Elise's furrowed brow that she was worried about her. Biting the inside of her cheek, Hayley sat back and looked down at the notepad on her lap. No sense in fighting for the article. She was, after all, the new kid. Technically, she should let Jill guide her instead of trying to make her mark from the very start.

"You came here to write about stuff that matters, right? Not bullshit peace and love stuff about the one-percenters who pretend to care and give their money to feminist causes, while still living the high life. But if you want to be put on a political beat right from the get-go, I have an assignment for you. That is, if you can handle it." Jill plucked a piece of paper off her desk and offered it to Hayley. "That McClusky asshole is looking to get re-elected yet again. He's been in the Senate since Nixon's time, for fuck's sake. Give our readership something on him, something to outrage them into voting against him. Career politicians are the reason we're so mired in outdated modes of thinking when it comes to women's rights. Urge our readers to get out there and make their voice heard."

"I…" Hayley looked at the paper and winced. It had a laundry list of McClusky's anti-woman bills and votes. There were many of them, more than she had expected. How did a guy like that raise an extraordinary woman like Veronica? "I'm sorry, but I went to school to be a serious journalist, not write exposes and hateful pieces about politicians, whatever their stances, whether I disagree with them or not. If I write something, it's going to be constructive, not destructive."

"Serious journalism." The set of Jill's jaw told Hayley she was just digging her own grave. "Don't you dare lecture me about serious journalism. Serious journalism, new girl, is telling people about this guy, making his voting record public knowledge so there is no doubt what he stands for or against. If you can't do it, then why the fuck are you here, Becker?"

Hayley clamped her lips together and kept her gaze lowered. Otherwise, she knew she would glare at Jill. She could probably stare a hole right through her tiny head if she tried hard enough. It was certainly a tempting thought. Jill hadn't come off so bitchy during the interview or first meeting. She was confident in those instances, and even sassy, but not snarky.

Dr. Jekyll/Mrs. Hyde. Great. Just what I always wanted in a boss when I've got so much to prove.

"Fine. You can't handle it. No worries. You'll learn to. For now, just stick with the perspectives column, girls."

The way Jill said "girls" rankled and Hayley felt white-hot rage fill her. *No. Fucking. Way.* She could hear her heartbeat thumping in her ears and she wondered if the rise and fall of her chest gave her anger away.

Jill went to yank the paper out of Hayley's hands, but Hayley jerked it away from her and held it close to her body. "No. I've got this." She had to because if she didn't write it, someone else would. Probably a more experienced staff writer with the same negative attitude as the editor-in-chief. And what would they say about Veronica's father? Or even about Veronica herself?

As they walked out of the meeting, Elise hissed, "What was that all about? And on our first full day, too. I love you and I think you're smart, but you are going to get yourself fired as fast as you got hired."

"Look, we came here to tell the truth, right? This is about realizing the people who represent us in Congress aren't the only ones who matter in this country, that the political elite aren't the only people with power. This is about the fact that there are other people out there making a difference," Hayley answered. "I want readers to see that they don't have to be rich and famous or hold office for their voices to matter."

"Girl, the only difference about to be made in your life is whether or not you're collecting a paycheck. Unemployment is a bitch. You don't want to go there."

Elise was right. Still, Hayley clung stubbornly to the paper. "I didn't get into journalism to fall into line and do whatever someone else wanted me to do. I'm here to tell people the truth. I'm writing this article on Senator McClusky," she answered. "I'll prove myself to Jill by making people want to get out and vote this year."

"Just as long as you don't make them want to vote for him."

Hayley sat at her desk without another word and glanced around the wide open office. Other writers were at their computers, typing away, getting work done. She and Elise were two of a handful of new college grads recently hired to work at the *Feminist Flag*. Like her, the other new hires looked more wide-eyed and uncertain than their more experienced counterparts, but just as determined to get the job done.

This was not her dream job. No. And she had accepted that when she took the job. Unfortunately, the environment was already far more cutthroat than she expected. What had she gotten herself into? Maybe she should have kept her mouth shut in that meeting. After all, she didn't know everything. Even as a college graduate, she still had a lot to learn. Too bad Jill wasn't exactly giving her the guidance and mentorship she expected from an editor.

With a quick peek to make sure Jill wasn't anywhere near the open workspace, let alone her desk, Hayley pulled out her phone and tapped it to check notifications. There was a text message from Veronica.

Thank goodness. Relief filled her and steadied her racing heart. The text message was something that put her back in touch with those new, wonderful feelings of love and freedom.

Are you having a good first day?

Hayley pursed her lips and pondered her response. Honesty was usually the best policy, but how was she going to tell the woman she was dating that she just sort of, kind of, accidentally-on-purpose took on an assignment to write a derogatory piece about her father… and convince people *not* to vote for him?

Not that Veronica would care, of course. Hayley knew she wouldn't vote for her own father, either. Still, it felt wrong to tell her about the assignment… and wrong not to.

Fighting the urge to thump her head against the desk a couple of times, Hayley texted back, *Oh yeah. It's fabulous. The editor-in-chief hates me already.*

In a minute, she received Veronica's reply. *That is fabulous, indeed! Let's celebrate evil bosses together. Want to go to a party with me tonight?*

On a Monday night? Hayley asked. She supposed she was an adult and didn't have to be prudish about partying on a weeknight. Then again, she realized Veronica's idea of a party was probably very different than an entire college dorm's...

Why not? Let's make today really outstanding. I need to be at a benefit for my father. Talk about evil! Come with me? I think I'm going to need a superhero.

Ouch.

The universe was officially out to get her.

✳✳✳

Hayley made it through her first day of work without getting fired. Elise was her saving grace. Somehow, her friend managed to pull the four columns she and Hayley had written together previously in college that she knew would make Jill salivate with glee.

"So we're revamping these, because the basic content is evergreen, always pertinent to women's rights,

especially the need for intersectional feminism. She
wants to run them in this order." Elise arranged the print-
outs on her desk for a visual and Hayley nodded after a
moment.

"How much freshening up do they need?"

"Well, since they were first printed in the
Georgetown Voice, technically a lot. I mean, first rights
were theirs, so that means we can use the basic ideas, but
we're going to have to change our presentation up a bit.
Still, if we consider that these particular columns were
written when we were sophomores and juniors, I bet
when we re-read them, we'll find our perspectives have
shifted at least somewhat. I think we will have a more
mature take on these topics now."

Hayley snagged an empty chair from a nearby desk
and wheeled it over so she could sit next to Elise. It took
an hour that afternoon to hash out the details of how they
could rewrite their columns and another hour to draft
outlines to work from.

"What's the deadline on the first one?" Hayley
asked, tapping her pencil against her notebook.

"She wants the first draft by Friday. Do you think

you can do it?"

Hayley nodded as she scanned her notes and then her outlines. "Yeah, I can."

"Even with the McClusky article? That's a pretty tall order." Elise spun in her chair and then faced Hayley. "Look, I know you wanted to write about politics, but can I just say I think that's a bad business? I think our concern should be more about empowering women and working on their mindset, not hate pieces."

"Trust me, I agree with you one hundred percent, which is why I pitched that article about the daughters. I thought it would empower our readers."

"But that was too fluffy. She hated it."

"Yeah." Hayley flipped back to her notes on the article she originally proposed. She already had a detailed outline on her laptop, written in a burst of inspiration on Sunday night. "I know she did. She made her feelings pretty clear."

Even though Elise looked sympathetic, she said firmly, "Jill wants the empowering articles, yeah, but with concrete steps toward progress and change. No, 'We're women, let's have sisterly love, rah, rah, rah' stuff, but more along the lines of what we were writing at the *Georgetown Voice*. She wants us to give women actions they can take to make a difference. I know you can give her what she wants, Hay. She wouldn't have hired you if you couldn't."

Hayley knew that, too. So how the heck was she going to spin the McClusky piece into something palatable enough for her to write, while still giving her editor what she wanted?

Despite the fact that Hayley rarely swore, she muttered, "Fuck my life," under her breath and closed her eyes.

"I know." Elise set her pen down and shook her head. "I thought I had it all figured out by college, that it would all be so easy from here on out. Like I was invincible or something. College was tough, but it sure as hell didn't prepare us for this."

"No, it sure as hell didn't." Hayley smoothed both of her hands back over her hair and hunched forward. "There was always that one professor we had to work our butts off to impress, to do well in his or her class. If this is what working with Jill is going to be like, I'm not sure I can handle it."

"And it's only the first day."

Hayley and Elise exchanged grim looks. "It's not like I expected life and work to be easy," Hayley hastened to add. She didn't want to sound like she was whining about something that was pretty normal in the world. "But I didn't expect to go from school to this kind of pressure."

"We knew journalism would be high pressure and I don't think that's the issue. I think the issue is that she's a bitch."

When Elise giggled, Hayley smiled. "Yeah, that's pretty much it. Only I was trying to be too nice to say it like that."

"Well, I guess we'll either get used to it or realize this isn't the place for us. Either way here's to working for a living."

Even though Elise was being sarcastic, Hayley wished she had something to at least raise in a mock toast. A cold drink sounded very appealing right now.

"To working for a living."

Chapter 11

"AND SHE BASICALLY TREATED me like a kid. I thought next time she opened her mouth, she'd breathe fire. Maybe roar a bit like the ferocious dragon lady she is. Holy crap, I do not want to go back there." Hayley lifted the wine glass to her lips as Veronica chuckled.

"Oh dear. This wouldn't have happened if you let me put in a word for you at the *Washington Post*. They love me over there."

"Mm." Hayley swallowed her wine and shook her head, pointing at Veronica as she did. "That's not necessarily true. They may love you, but there are scary bosses everywhere, even at a place as prestigious as the *Post*. In fact, it's probably more prevalent there. But I'm a big girl and I'll learn how to deal with mine."

"I know you will. Prove her wrong. And speaking of bosses, my father is walking this way." Veronica's eyes narrowed before she turned and smoothed her hands down the front of her black dress. "How do I look?"

Hayley sighed as her gaze raked Veronica from head to toe. The blonde looked gorgeous, of course, wearing a tasteful black evening gown. "You look perfect, of course. You always do."

"You're sweet. But you look amazing too, so don't flatter me." Veronica patted Hayley's cheek and her gaze wandered down, tracing the lines of Hayley's evening gown. It was as if they had made physical contact. Hayley felt her nipples bud beneath the fabric and a shiver ran through her. She supposed her dress looked fine, even if it was an inexpensive formal dress from the juniors section at the local department store. She'd purchased it for college soirees and worn it only a few times. The floor-length white sheath looked good on her, but it was definitely not some fancy label.

Veronica sparkled in the lighting of the ballroom, while Hayley felt as though she faded into the background. That was fine with her, though. She didn't want to draw attention to herself. As far as she was concerned, she was there to support Veronica through a party she had no desire to attend.

Most of the people were here to donate money to Veronica's father's campaign for re-election. Or at least that was Senator McClusky's hope. The majority of the people here would be perfect fodder for an outrageous article for the *Feminist Flag*. In fact, Jill would probably blow her stack if she knew Hayley was here *not* taking notes on the entire evening – who was who, what they said, and what they did. It was a who's who of conservative Washington businessmen and lobbyists.

But Hayley couldn't help that there was a huge difference between writing a piece as a call to action and writing one as a scathing expose. Taking Veronica's father down was the last thing she wanted to do, whether she agreed with his politics or not.

"Hey, can we talk?" Hayley asked.

"In a minute. Here he comes." Veronica squirmed a bit and then straightened her shoulders. "The old man prides himself on thinking I'm the perfect daughter. I still don't have the heart to break it to him that I'm far from it."

Hayley wanted to point out that odds were Veronica's father knew she wasn't perfect and that it didn't matter if he loved her. She held her tongue, though, because in another moment a much-older man in a tuxedo was standing in front of them, kissing Veronica on the cheek.

"Dad," she said with a smile, "what a wonderful night. I see you have a wonderful turnout and everything is lovely."

"Thank you, Veronica. Won't you introduce me to your guest? You never bring friends to these events."

Veronica turned to Hayley with a smile. "I decided I needed someone interesting to talk to. Your cronies don't count."

Both father and daughter laughed, but Hayley wasn't sure it was all that funny. She wanted to melt into the woodwork and slink out of the room.

"Anyway, Dad, this is Hayley Becker. She's a recent graduate of Georgetown University."

"Georgetown? My, my. Are you from any Beckers I would know?" the senator asked as he shook Hayley's hand.

"No, definitely not," Hayley said.

"Well, you are still quite welcome to my party, Hayley. What's your major?"

Hayley felt a cold chill shake her as the senator's rough, papery-skinned hand continued to clasp hers.

"Liberal arts with a minor in journalism," she answered. "I want to be a journalist."

"Now, I hope you didn't take a job at the *Washington Post* with those liberal media yahoos." Even though he sounded good-natured and winked at her, the senator grasped her hand a little tighter before letting it go.

"No, though I have to admit I interviewed there. I'm..." Hayley smiled uneasily. "I'm still trying to find my fit." It was a little white lie, but it rolled off her tongue as if it were the truth. After all, she was still trying to figure out her place at the *Flag* and as a journalist in general.

"Well, if you need any recommendations, let me know."

Veronica steered her father away from Hayley with a whispered, "By the way, how is Mom doing?"

Grateful for the rescue, Hayley finished off her wine and then reached for another as a waiter walked past her. It was her first time being on this side of the serving tray and it felt a little... off. This wasn't the world for her. And if she didn't feel comfortable here, how was she going to make it journalism? She supposed she might feel different if she was dressed for work and attending as a writer, not as a guest. Ask questions and find a story, she could do. But mingling with the rich and powerful? So not her thing.

Being alone with Veronica – just the two of them in a fancy restaurant or her beautiful townhouse – was different. When they were alone together, it was like being in their own safe, lovely world.

"Okay, I'm back." Veronica gave her one of those wide, sincere smiles that made Hayley go shivery all over. She couldn't deny the desire that pooled inside her, that made her ache for Veronica and all that she was. Beautiful, outgoing, spontaneous. All the things Hayley was not, but wondered if she could learn to be.

"Veronica…"

"Oh, no." Veronica reached out to grasp her upper arms and looked at her with concern in her eyes. "You look a little pale. I'm sorry. You're finding this very uncomfortable, aren't you?"

"Not uncomfortable. Just…" Hayley wanted to tear her gaze away from Veronica, to look around the room and see if the right word came to mind, but she couldn't.

The grip on her arms tightened a little, enough to let her know Veronica had every intention of making her leave the room – probably the party. "We can't have that. I'm so sorry I invited you here. I didn't want to be here either, but I thought having you with me would make it easier. It was selfish of me. Come on. We can leave now that I've made an appearance and talked to my father. Let's get out of here."

Even though Hayley hadn't said a word, Veronica swept her out of the fancy ballroom, out of the house, and to her waiting car. In only fifteen minutes they had ditched the party and were walking in downtown D.C. in their evening gowns, eating ice cream.

"Now this is a date," Veronica declared as she licked some of the vanilla dripping off her cone.

Hayley smiled and said, "I can't believe you like boring vanilla ice cream." Her own cone was pretty hefty with a combination of cookies and cream and rocky road piled on it.

"Vanilla isn't boring," Veronica answered. "It's classic. It will never let you down. There's nothing wrong with having something safe and reliable, like a beautiful Midwestern girlfriend."

"Girlfriend?" Hayley stopped and turned to Veronica, reaching out to take her hand. It was the first time she'd extended a romantic gesture on her own without any prompting. All she wanted to do was touch Veronica, to assure herself she was real. "Am I your girlfriend?"

"For tonight, at least." The way Veronica accepted her hand, turned their palms to press together, and then laced her fingers through Hayley's was a deliciously intimate gesture. Suddenly, Hayley wanted Veronica more than she wanted the double scoop of ice cream.

They still had to talk, though. Frustration and fear roiled in her gut. What was she supposed to say? She had gotten herself into her own predicament, she knew, and no amount of explaining would appease Veronica. How could it? In a town where everyone viewed everyone else with suspicion, there was no way Veronica would buy her explanations.

What could she say, anyway? *"I'm writing an expose about your father for my new job because I managed to back myself into a corner there."*

Veronica seemed to misinterpret her expression for concern about their relationship, because she said, "I'm kidding. You know that. I mean I'd like to date you and only you, Hayley, preferably for a very long time."

And then the senator's daughter leaned in to kiss her. Those lips of hers tasted just like vanilla ice cream and her tongue, when it entered Hayley's mouth, did too.

They let go of one another's hands only to tangle them in each other's hair, instead. Hayley wondered how they looked, standing there in party dresses, each holding an ice cream cone in one hand as they embraced passionately with the other. If anyone was going to take blackmail photos of Veronica, this would be the time to do it, Hayley thought wildly.

But there were no camera clicks, no scurrying feet.

There was just the two of them in this time and place. Together.

"Hey," Veronica said as they parted, "come spend the night at my place."

"I... work... tomorrow. Tomorrow is work." Hayley couldn't think straight and she blinked to make sure the world around her was real.

"Then can I stay over at your place? You've got that bed now and we still haven't tested it."

Veronica was right. The bed remained chaste. Hayley nodded and it wasn't long before they found themselves in her apartment.

The furnishings were still sparse, but it had only been a few days since she moved in. Hayley needed time to settle into her new job before she worried about decorating the apartment. At least she had what mattered and the lack of furniture didn't seem to bother Veronica. The statuesque blonde sauntered across the living room, her heels clacking against the hardwood floor. Then she stood there at the bare window, looking through it.

"Do you know why I love my townhouse?" she asked without looking at Hayley. "It's because of the view. Here you can only see the building across the street, but I can see the entire city skyline from my living room. The lights at night are spectacular. It's the reason I love cities. Sure, all of us are concentrated in one place – a crowd of people and buildings and all the crap that comes with that. But at night when you look outside from a building that's tall enough or far enough away, the lights are amazing."

She turned around and gave Hayley a smile, before sauntering back toward her.

"That's pretty cool if you think about it – how everything sort of quiets down at night in a place like this, and is peaceful and luminous. You know?"

Hayley knew, but she didn't say anything. Instead, she reached out and cupped the back of Veronica's head before lowering hers to claim a kiss. This was her girlfriend and she was going to make love to her all night long. Who cared that she had to get up early and go to work? Veronica was here, in her apartment, and ready to be loved.

The way Veronica's lips moved beneath hers was intoxicating and Hayley had to have her. She guided her back into the bedroom and instead of hitting the bed, they ended up against the wall. It didn't matter, she decided. All that mattered was her hands and lips on this gorgeous woman.

She wanted so badly to touch her, but that evening gown… The sparkles on it caught on her hands every time she tried to run them up along Veronica's body. So

Hayley reached around with both arms and found the zipper. She drew it down as slowly as she could. As much as she wanted to see Veronica step out of the black dress and offer herself, Hayley also wanted to tease her.

It must have been working because Veronica moaned against her mouth and curled her fingers into her hips as if urging her to move faster. When the zipper could descend no further, Hayley took several steps back and said, "Undress for me."

For once in her life, Veronica didn't answer back. She simply moved her hands up to the shoulders of the dress and moved it down along her arms, letting it fall to the ground. Underneath it, she was as beautiful as ever. Her compact body was covered only in a black lacy bra and panties now, and a pair of black stockings.

She was like a pin-up come to life. Not as young or curvy as most, but still beautiful, still seductive and inviting as she stood there looking confident.

Hayley stepped forward again and took Veronica's hands. She pressed them back against the wall and tilted her head to nibble at that slim, graceful neck. Veronica's skin vibrated beneath her lips as she moaned. With a smile, Hayley lowered her face to nuzzle at Veronica's breasts. The way her nipples hardened into stiff peaks invited Hayley to play with them, to kiss them through the sheer fabric and then bite gently at them.

Veronica let out a hiss of need and arched her back. "Hayley," she whispered.

But Hayley carried on as if she hadn't said anything. She focused on loving those breasts, stroking and caressing them without touching any other part of her girlfriend's body. Before long, Veronica was mewling at her, sometimes begging her to work her way lower, to make her orgasm.

Hayley didn't tell her she would do that when she was good and ready, though. She just took her time, giving her full attention to that soft, warm flesh. When she finally dipped her fingers down into Veronica's panties, she found them soaking with the evidence of her lust.

Wanting to give her girlfriend the same intense pleasure Veronica had given her the first two times they had sex, Hayley kept her pinned against the wall and knelt before her. With her nose, she managed to push the flimsy material of her panties aside.

And with her tongue, she made Veronica scream with ecstasy again and again that night.

Chapter 12

The article was not going well.

Hayley stared at her screen and blew out a breath of frustration. She already knew Jill was going to hate it because it was pretty much a flimsy piecing together of the facts she already had. The article so far talked about McClusky's voting record and bills, yes, but it had a much softer tone than Hayley knew Jill wanted from her.

She leaned back in her chair and glared at the calendar. It was already Friday. Her first week at work felt like it was teetering on the edge of failure.

Together, she and Elise had turned in their first rewritten column earlier in the week and Jill loved it. Gushed over it, even, saying how this was exactly the kind of thing the *Feminist Flag* needed. And then she'd fixed Hayley with a stare and asked her how the McClusky piece was coming.

It wasn't coming along at all. It was floundering, flailing as badly as Hayley had flailed through her first week. Her only saving grace was Elise, who drew Jill's focus back to their shared perspectives column with an idea for where they could bring it in the future.

Now that Hayley was staring at the McClusky piece again, she knew there was no way she could make the article sound the way Jill wanted. Hayley just couldn't do hateful, even if someone deserved it. She would much rather encourage people to vote for the ones who could make a change than discourage them from voting for the ones who wouldn't. Even though she knew anger would incite action, she wondered if there was a better way.

"Hey, girl." Elise slid onto her desk and raised her hands in the air. "You're working too hard. Let's go to lunch to celebrate surviving our first week."

Hayley tore her tired, watering eyes away from the screen and looked at her friend. Survival. That was the right word for it.

"Jeez, you look awful. Are you getting any sleep?" Elise leaned forward and inspected her face. "Or are you about to cry?"

"No and yes." Hayley plucked a tissue out of the box on her desk and swiped at her eyes harder than she intended. "Shit. Tissue touched my eye. Damn it!"

Elise stifled a laugh. "I think I've heard you swear

more times in one week here than I ever did in four years of college. That can't be a good sign. My innocent Midwestern friend has fallen victim to the Dark Side of journalistic pressure."

"Yeah, maybe. I just don't know what I'm going to…" Hayley blew out a breath as her vision sharpened. Elise was smart. Maybe she could help Hayley figure out what to do. So as soon as finished blinking the extra tears out of her eye and ditched the offending tissue, Hayley scooped her purse out of her desk drawer and said, "Let's go."

When they were settled in at a small, trendy café not far from their offices, Hayley decided to lay it out for Elise. She told her everything – about her relationship with Veronica and the problem the article represented, the party, and even meeting Veronica's father. When she was done explaining her predicament, she waited. During the conversation, Elise had asked some questions and Hayley had watched her eyes go from narrow to wide to narrow again. That was one thing she could really count on with Elise. She *listened* and she was bound to have shrewd advice for her.

"So, what do you think about this mess?" Hayley asked.

Elise pursed her lips. "I think," she said after a long pause, "that you're highly fucked, my friend."

"Well, thanks. That's helpful." They stared at each other and finally erupted into giggles. Even Hayley couldn't help but thump the table as she chortled and Elise snorted.

Their waiter barely spared them a glance as he set their sandwiches down and walked away without asking if they needed anything else.

"But seriously, you're in a hard place, it seems," Elise said as she squirted ketchup on the plate next to her fries. "This is an obvious conflict of interest. If you're going to stay in journalism, dating a politician's daughter isn't a good idea. If you're going to keep dating her, journalism might not be the right career for you. What are you going to do about it?"

"I don't know." Hayley stared down at her patty melt. It smelled heavenly. Sure, she'd have to brush her teeth after eating a sandwich loaded with onions, but one bite and she knew it was worth it. For a moment, she toyed with the idea of walking up to Jill and sharing her onion breath with the one person she couldn't stand.

"I guess the question is what's more important to you – your job or your relationship. Considering you've wanted to be a journalist since you were a kid and are realizing now how much you like being in love, it's a hard question."

Hayley covered her mouth as she chewed while the gears in her mind started turning. Leave it to Elise to ask the hard questions. Though, that was one of the reasons why Hayley loved her. Elise was always straightforward, no-BS, and got to the heart of the matter. Hayley suspected that was part of her upbringing as the granddaughter of people who had to fight for basic civil rights. Speak your truth. Elise was good at that, as well as mirroring it to others.

"At this point, it's hard to say," Hayley finally answered. "I'm just getting established in my career. One wrong move could kill it."

"And you're relationship is still new, too, but you're in love. I have a feeling you're going to need some mouth-to-mouth before it's all said and done."

Even though Elise was trying to be humorous, Hayley's mouth barely twitched. She just nodded and took a drink of her soda. "I just want it all," she said. "I want to have both, but if the career is going to conflict with the relationship, I'm going to have to make a choice."

"Something you didn't want to acknowledge, but you're kind of being forced to now," Elise observed. "Did you realize you should have thought about that before choosing to date someone like Veronica?"

"Oh yes, very much so." Hayley stared at the sandwich, trying to think of an answer. "Is it bad of me to say I don't know which is more important right now?"

"No. I'm pretty sure it's human nature to want both. You've always been ambitious and wanted to succeed, but now that you have the love you've denied yourself, you want that too. I suppose it would be kind of shitty to put your career before another human being."

Hayley grimaced. That was harsh, but Elise was probably correct. "Even another human I hardly know."

"I wouldn't say you hardly know her. You know her well enough to refer to her as your girlfriend, to have dated her for the past month, to have slept with her a few times already. So there's obviously something there."

Elise was right yet again. There was definitely something there. Hayley wouldn't be with Veronica if there wasn't, especially considering she'd avoided dating for so long.

"If you decided she's the right person and this is the right time, you don't want to mess it up."

Ducking her head, Hayley stared down at her sandwich and then took another bite of it. What could she possibly say to that? Elise hit the nail on the head again. "Job," she said after she swallowed her food. "What do I do about that?"

"You either come clean with Veronica about the article or you tell Jill you just can't do it."

"So those are my options? They both kind of suck."

Elise rested her chin on her hand and stared at her, those brown eyes full of sympathy even as she gave Hayley the tough love she needed. "What I think sucks is keeping a secret from someone you love. Why don't you tell me what sucks about telling Veronica the truth?"

"Well, everything. She might not believe me or she

might lose her trust in me. That's something I can't deal with right now. Meeting Veronica is like discovering another way to live, you know? She's spontaneous and open and fun. She's all the things I'm not, but at the same time, she's just as uptight as I am. Do you know what I mean?"

"Sort of. So, what sucks about telling Jill you can't do it?"

The thought sent a curl of cold fear into Hayley's stomach and she shuddered visibly. "Besides the way she'll sneer at me, call me a *girl*, inform me that I can't hack it, and tell me to get my ass back to the minor leagues?"

"Right." Elise nodded and then poked at her French fries. "You really are stuck between a rock and a hard place. I guess what you need to do is figure out what's important to you – your job or your relationship like I said."

"There must be a way to write the article that makes Jill happy and keeps Veronica from finding out, or at least isn't pissy enough to upset her."

"Well, you said Veronica doesn't agree with her

father's politics anyway, so I vote for telling her the truth about it. Besides, if you write it behind her back, odds are she'll hear about it one way or another. And if your byline is on it..." Elise shrugged and picked up a fry. "Your ass will be grass then."

And that was that for the bitch session. Hayley didn't know if it made her dilemma better or worse. Everything seemed the same and that wasn't good. At least Elise had asked the one question she needed to consider: job or relationship? Which did she value more?

Hayley knew it was crappy of her to choose her job, particularly a job she wasn't happy with, over her girlfriend. She also knew Veronica would never want to stand in the way of her career. Even though she couldn't foresee the future of her relationship, it tugged at her heart more than the idea of keeping her job did. Besides, her future with the *Feminist Flag* already seemed pretty darn shaky. With no way of knowing which would endure, she was left with the unanswered question.

As they walked back to the office, Elise finally offered her opinion. "Look, I don't want to influence you, but if it were me, I'd choose the girlfriend over the job. Even if it goes wrong someday, at least you know you had someone to love you for a while, you know? Your job is never going to love you back. Jobs are easier to find than love. Trust me on that."

"Yeah, I know where you're coming from." Hayley let out a sigh and flashed her ID at the security guard in the lobby. Jabbing at the button in the elevator was only slightly satisfying. It was tearing Hayley up inside to realize the situation she was in – choosing between her lifelong dream and the woman she had only recently met.

When they were back at their desks, Hayley looked at her half-written article and then slowly typed at the top of it "A Vote for Love." The title would piss Jill off and that was the best part of it. Other than that, Hayley had a feeling Jill was going to reject the article no matter how she wrote it.

She'd have to tell Veronica about the article sooner or later, she decided. Even if her bitchy editor was unlikely to publish the article, Hayley wanted Veronica to know about it. The whole reason she got into journalism was because she believed in upholding the integrity of freedom of the press.

Now that she was back in the office, Hayley decided all she could do was focus on her work. She opened Google and ran a search for the woman running against McClusky for the same Senate seat. With two screens open, she worked her way between the existing information and her own article. As she added sentences about the woman seeking the Senate seat in hopes of upsetting the incumbent, Hayley didn't feel better. But she did feel productive.

The facts she found didn't give her much hope. The woman was a relative unknown in politics, other than on a very low local level. But she'd done well in her previous positions and her stance certainly seemed to align with what the *Feminist Flag* stood for – women first.

After pondering her dry article, Hayley glanced at the clock. It was nearly the end of the day. She decided her best option was to sleep on it and come back to it on Monday. Maybe inspiration would strike over the weekend. Maybe she would work up the courage to tell Veronica about it. Maybe there would stop being so darn many maybes in her life.

She opened her purse and checked her phone.

I've got another family favor to ask – dinner with the parents tonight. I know it's short notice and you can say no, but I wanted to ask.

Hayley blinked a few times at the text. For someone who tried awful hard to hide her romantic relationships from her father, Veronica certainly seemed to be failing at it. Unless she was inviting Hayley to dinner in another capacity?

That didn't seem likely, though. Who brought a friend to dinner with their family, unless it was a long-time friend?

Still, an idea sparked in Hayley's mind. Another maybe.

Maybe she could somehow get an informal interview out of the deal. After all, dinner wasn't like a party, where McClusky had to make sure he spoke with everyone there. This was a chance for a one-on-one conversation with the man she was writing about. She might be able to get something she could use in the article, something that would make it much more interesting than what she had at the moment.

But if even the slightest gist of the conversation ended up in her article, as it probably would, Veronica would recognize it. That meant Hayley had to come clean with her before publication if publication happened. Heck, she had to say something even before submitting the article to her editor. Before dinner, if possible.

No, there was no time to talk before dinner, because Veronica texted again to say *It's at 6 p.m. Just let me know and I'll pick you up at 5:30.*

Hayley took a deep breath, both her thumbs poised over the screen of her phone. She was about to do something that was either very brave or very stupid. Whether or not she threw away her relationship or her career hinged on tonight.

Yes, she texted back. *Heading home now to change.*

In a few moments, she got her tongue-in-cheek answer.

Don't change. I love you just the way you are.

Chapter 13

THE SWANKY RESTAURANT WAS like something out of a movie and being with the senator was surreal.

Hayley tried not to think about it too much, but inside she was freaking out. Hard. It wasn't the man himself. He was a pompous windbag, she learned soon enough. It was the fact that, once again, she found herself on the other side of the serving tray in a place with low lights, soft music, men in suits, and women in dresses.

Not only that, but she realized she was looking at some of D.C.'s crème de la crème sitting at the tables. Republicans, Democrats, journalists, and other movers and shakers filled the restaurant.

How Veronica intended to keep their relationship quiet was beyond Hayley. This was their second appearance together in the presence of her father. There was no way he was going to believe Hayley was just a friend, and that's what worried her even more.

After small talk and the salad course, her fear gave way to curiosity. That same curiosity that was a part of what drove her into journalism kicked in and she leaned over to say to the senator's wife, "I'm sorry I missed you at the party on Monday, but it was such a pleasure to be there."

The wife smiled. She was a nervous-looking woman, her disposition fidgety and her blue eyes watery. Her black hair was laced with gray and styled in a short perm. "My health doesn't always allow me to be at every event, but I try when I can."

It was then that Hayley realized Veronica resembled neither the senator nor his wife. She scanned their faces, trying to be subtle, before returning her attention to Mrs. McClusky. "Well, I hope you feel well enough to be here tonight."

"I do, dear." The woman didn't look well at all. Beneath her make-up she was pale, her cheeks looking more rouged than natural. Hayley thought she really ought to be resting, not out having dinner.

"She feels well when it suits her," Senator McClusky boomed out and Hayley saw his wife flinch. "So, Hayley, have you found a job yet? I know it's only been a week, but there are plenty of opportunities here for a talented young college graduate."

Hayley curled her hand around her water glass, feeling its smooth surface slip beneath her fingers. There was a slight narrowing of Veronica's eyes as if she were waiting to pounce. Like her father, no doubt, but not in the same direction.

"Actually, yes. I'm working," Hayley said, recalling one of the lessons her girlfriend had taught her. In a city where information is power, don't give too much of either one away.

"And may I ask where?"

Sipping at her water, Hayley tried not to think too hard about the question. She couldn't let it throw her, couldn't let herself be bothered by the senator's response, whatever it might be. "Sure, I'm at the *Feminist Flag* as a staff writer."

The senator chuckled, his body shaking with laughter. "Oh, that little piss-ant internet rag. There's more and more of them these days. Don't put all your eggs in one basket, Hayley. They won't last. None of the others have."

"Then what do you suggest?" Hayley knew it was

daring to ask, but she wanted to hear the senator's perspective.

"I suggest if you want to write the truth, you get to the heart of it yourself. Not write for some jackass with an agenda."

Veronica's hand lifted as if she was going to place it on her father's arm. Watching that hand, Hayley said, "But aren't we all jackasses with an agenda?"

The hand stopped, Veronica drew it off the table, and the senator looked taken aback by Hayley's candid response.

"I mean, we are in Washington D.C., Senator, and if you're here, it's because you have a reason. For you, it's to push your agenda of so-called 'family values'. For some of us, it's to reveal the truth. So it's hardly fair to make that judgment of where I work or what anyone here does when we're all doing the same thing."

The senator turned to Veronica and patted her upper arm. "Oh, she's a keeper, Ronnie. She's a keeper. Smart, pretty, and knows how to play the game."

"Don't call me Ronnie," Veronica muttered, withdrawing from her father's patting hand. "And of course she's a keeper. I don't make friends with idiots."

Now her father's laughter turned to sputtering. "Friends. Please. I've known since you were a teenager the last thing you wanted with other girls was friendship. But as long as you've kept it quiet, it hasn't been a problem."

He... knew? Of course he did and Hayley wasn't surprised.

Senator McClusky turned back to Hayley. "Not that I condone it, of course. There's no excuse, not even for pretty ladies to have sexual relations with each other. It's distasteful and the only thing it can possibly do is weaken the family unit. Women are meant to get married and have babies, and they can't do that with each other."

The man was still shaking with mirth as if the very thought of women doing anything other than getting married and having children was ridiculous.

Hayley glanced at Veronica, who looked at a loss for once. Then she looked at the senator's wife, whose head was bowed, gnarled hand fluttering toward her wineglass.

After committing the quote to memory, Hayley

looked back at the senator and shrugged. "And that's just one person's opinion, Senator," she said.

"That's the opinion of many of my constituents. Besides, it's based on the Good Book." He looked triumphant as if he had somehow managed to win a fight, even though there was none.

"You know, coming from the Midwest, I was raised to believe in the Bible, too." Hayley leaned back in her chair, warming up to her subject. Somehow her confidence was rising. Like the confidence she'd had all through high school and college, her belief that she could face anything and master it.

"Good. I'm glad your parents taught you well. But you know the tenets of the Bible mean your relationship with my daughter is against everything God stood for."

Hayley tilted her head and smiled. "I didn't say I agree completely with it, but that's how it goes, right? Our parents raise us the way they think is best and then we grow up and figure things out for ourselves. That's not to say I don't believe in God or Jesus. I do. But I also think love is the least of the sins I could possibly commit."

"That's awfully presumptuous, girl." The senator didn't sound so amused anymore.

"I know, but let he who is without sin cast the first stone." Hayley thought about the senator's voting record and other things she had dug up on him in the course of her research. It wasn't much, but it was enough to drive her next point home. "As far as I know, gay relationships aren't forbidden by the Ten Commandments, but I've been pretty good about avoiding stealing and adultery, not to mention bearing false witness. So I'll let God judge me, not you."

She saw Senator McClusky's knuckles tighten and she wondered if he would ask her what she was accusing him of. But he didn't give her that satisfaction. Instead, he loosened his hand and chortled. "One of those New Agey 'Jesus is love' types, eh?"

"More like someone who realizes I can only do the best I can with the life I have and I'm not going to be so arrogant as to think I can judge others. I'll leave that to a higher power, so excuse me if I don't acknowledge you as God, Senator."

It certainly wasn't the most rational argument Hayley

had ever made and it wasn't the most informed one, either. She wasn't exactly a fallen-away Christian, but she wasn't a studious one. She just knew her beliefs were her own and she wasn't about to take any crap from a man whose entire life revolved around putting his judgment on others while taking campaign donations from special interests with conflicting agendas.

But she also wasn't going to put her knowledge out there, either. No. She would save that for her article and see how the self-righteous senator felt once it was on the internet for everyone to see.

Because knowledge was power and something told her there was more of a story beneath all of this.

***

"I'm sorry about my father," Veronica said as the driver brought them back to Hayley's apartment. "He's such a jerk, but you did a good job. I've never been able to throw his religious arguments back at him. It's just not something I know much about."

"Well, I didn't want to throw anything back at him, especially religion," Hayley answered. She was holding Veronica's hand, fingers tangled together, and snuggling up to her side. "My beliefs are my own and they are personal for me. I hate using them to fight because you can't win an argument with belief. That's why I didn't get deep into a Biblical discussion with him. Anyone can pick and choose a passage out of that to suit their beliefs and desires, but it won't change anyone's mind. And with him as your father, how could you not have some way to argue religious views with him? Didn't he raise you with the same beliefs as him?"

"Oh, Hayley... It's more complicated than that." Veronica looked away, her gaze on the window or something beyond it. "That's the trick, isn't it – changing minds?"

"Yeah." Hayley rubbed her other hand along Veronica's arm. "I'm not here to change minds, though. I'm here because I want people to know the truth. Veronica, that's what I need to talk to you about tonight."

She sat upright, pulling slightly away from her girlfriend. She had to tell her about the article. This was the moment.

"The truth." Veronica also straightened and looked at

her. "The truth is I love you, Hayley. I've dated many women and it's been fun but, damn, I really love you. I don't want any more fun in my life. I just want you."

A long silence extended between them until Veronica frayed it with a laugh.

"That sounded wrong. I mean, I do want to have fun, but you're the only person I want to have fun with. Does that make sense?"

Hayley nodded. "It does," she said softly. "I love you too."

"Good." Veronica leaned in for a kiss, but Hayley stopped her.

"But please let me talk to you first. I have something I have to say."

Veronica settled back and looked at her. "This sounds serious."

The way Hayley's heart thumped in her chest at those words, she thought she would keel over. But she managed to swallow a breath and nod. "It is because it's about truth and integrity and… Jeez, Veronica, I cornered myself at work on my first day there and I wanted to tell you, but I've been nervous. But I can't live with myself if I do this and the article goes to press, and then you see it or hear about it secondhand. So I have to tell you."

Veronica's eyes narrowed slightly and she nodded. "Go on."

"I pitched a story to my editor – one about you and women like you. I didn't name you or anything, but I wanted to write an inspiring piece about women making a difference in D.C. Not politicians, but women connected to them, you know?"

"I'm flattered."

Hayley's throat went dry and no matter how much she swallowed, she couldn't seem to get it moist again. "Thanks. If she accepted the pitch, I was going to ask you if I could write about you, among others. But she mocked it and told me if I really want to write something worthwhile, I could do a piece about your father exposing his voting record and anything else that will incite our readers to make sure they get out and vote against him. She questioned my commitment to journalism, so I accepted the assignment."

She saw Veronica's lips part just a bit but then close

again. Instead, her girlfriend gave another tight nod and waited.

"My editor wants me to write about his voting record and any other crap I can dig up on him, and I have dug it up. I mean, wow, have I found things that suck about him. But it's not scandalous by any means. No affairs, no bribes, no taking what he shouldn't. Just some campaign donations from lobbyists who represent a conflict of interest. Still, I can't write it and give it to my editor without telling you and asking if it's okay."

"Hayley…" Veronica lifted her hand and then settled it on Hayley's cheek. "Of course it's okay. It's your job and I'm not going to stand in the way of that. You aren't harming me and, really, you aren't harming my family. My father is so entrenched in politics here, the odds of him losing his seat to the woman running against him are low. I wish there was a way to get more voters out there, but I can't think of it. Believe me, I've tried. It's another cause I'm involved in – voter education, especially for the most disempowered people in our country."

As before when she learned unexpected things about her girlfriend, Hayley's heart swelled with pride. She could imagine Veronica talking one-on-one with a struggling farmer or coal miner, trying to explain why their voice mattered, even if they felt like it didn't.

"I'm sorry for not telling you sooner," she said.

An almost sad smile lifted the corners of Veronica's lips. "It's fine. I wish you had told me sooner, yes, but not for the sake of my family or something. I wish you'd told me because I wish you trusted me."

Trust. That had been Hayley's fear, that Veronica wouldn't trust her. But it really did go both ways. She knew that now and she nodded to acknowledge it. Grateful that they understood each other better, Hayley wrapped her arms around Veronica for a hug and sighed.

"I don't think my editor will take it when it's done, though. I just can't make it sound all that interesting. There's nothing new in there, nothing that will really outrage readers or make the article particularly interesting enough to share."

Veronica gave a little "hmph" next to her ear and as Hayley got out of the car, said, "By the way."

Hayley hesitated on the sidewalk and looked in the car at her girlfriend.

"You should do more digging if you want to make the article really stand out," Veronica continued, "because it would be interesting for the public to hear that Senator women-need-to-get-married-and-have-babies isn't married to my mother. He's married to her sister."

Chapter 14

SURELY WHAT VERONICA MEANT was her father had been married to her mother at one point, Hayley reasoned, married and then widowed. Or divorced. One or the other after Veronica's birth. And then he married the sister, Veronica's aunt because… well, because he wanted to keep the family together.

Yes, that had to be it.

Either way, it wasn't all that important, was it? Veronica's mother's and aunt's maiden name was Stone, no matter what, regardless of which one was married to the senator.

Right?

Those questions kept Hayley tossing and turning that night. When she woke up and crossed her empty apartment early on Saturday morning, she couldn't help but wonder if she should even bother to furnish it. At this rate, she wasn't going to survive in this town. Her dreams were coming crashing down all around her. Even with a wonderful girlfriend, going home was looking better and better at the moment.

But why had Veronica said what she said? Was she trying to throw her a bone? Hayley didn't need any favors. Yes, she loved Veronica, but what kind of journalist was she if she couldn't figure stuff out for herself? Sure, in the movies and TV shows, many reporters worked their contacts for information, but Hayley didn't want to be like that. Did she?

After her first cup of coffee, and reminding herself she needed a larger coffee maker, Hayley sat down on her bed and opened her laptop. She had emailed herself the article, just in case she felt like she could work on it over the weekend. It stared back at her, a limp mess of facts and flimsy sentences connecting them to the lobbyists' campaign donations. Not earth-shattering news. Nope. Just another politician fulfilling the "you scratch my back, I'll scratch yours" status quo.

She didn't edit the article with any notes from the previous night, though. Instead, she ran another Google search on Senator McClusky. Five pages into the results and she still didn't see anything to support Veronica's statement about her mother.

Hayley chewed at the inside of her cheek and then

blew a long breath out of her nose. Veronica was forty, which meant she was born in the seventies. Where was she born? Hayley went to the Wikipedia page for Veronica Stone-McClusky and read over it. She was born right there in D.C. Her father was already a senator, so there must have been a birth announcement.

A search of newspapers did yield a birth announcement, but it showed the senator's current wife, Patty, looking much younger and healthier than she did now. She held the baby, her face a mixture of fear and excitement.

And next to her was...

Hayley peered closely at the newspaper photo.

The other woman in the photo was Pamela Stone, Patty's sister, the senator's sister-in-law, and therefore Veronica's aunt.

Looking at Pamela was like seeing a 1977 version of an adult Veronica. She had the same sculpted eyebrows and wavy blonde hair, and she smirked at the camera slightly. It was the face of a beautiful woman with a story to tell.

What had Veronica said when they were first dating?

She used her mother's maiden name "because of reasons."

She followed in her mother's footsteps, but she never told Hayley what her mother did.

Hayley ran a new Google search for Pamela Stone and there she was – a model popular in the 1960s and 1970s. There were photos of her with such icons as Mick Jagger, Warren Beatty, and even Andy Warhol.

"Holy shit…" The truth of Veronica's parentage was there in black and white 1977 newsprint for everyone to see, so how come no one had made the connection?

Because they had bigger fish to fry in 1977, of course, like recovering from Vietnam and the ongoing marches for Civil Rights. Who would remember or care about the birth of a senator's daughter? And then who would bother to take the time fifteen years later to compare Veronica to her mother and aunt? And if they did, would they simply say she took after her aunt, rather than assuming she was actually her aunt's daughter? Genetics like that could have come from a grandparent, after all.

It was a leap of logic without proof, that was for

sure. The only way to prove Veronica was not Patty's daughter, but Pamela's was with a birth certificate. And who was to say Senator McClusky hadn't managed to ensure the birth certificate said his wife's name, instead of his sister-in-law's? DNA was a possibility, Hayley supposed, but considering Patty and Pamela were sisters, wouldn't they share the same mitochondrial DNA? And didn't that mean Veronica would, too? Hayley didn't know enough about DNA to answer that question. It seemed like all she had to rely on were firsthand accounts – daughter, mother, and maybe hospital personnel.

Again, the questions went round and round, as someone knocked on Hayley's door.

Hayley slid off the bed and crossed her apartment, stopping only to pour the second cup of coffee that was hot and ready. When she opened the door, Veronica was standing there in blue jeans and a white t-shirt and wearing comically oversized sunglasses.

"So, I hear a reporter wants to interview me to get to the heart of the story," she said, tossing her hair and tilting her head back as if looking up at the ceiling.

"Veronica…" Hayley leaned against the door. "I can't do that to you."

"Do what to me – accept that I've come willingly to share my mother's story with you?" Veronica shrugged and drew the sunglasses off her face. "Look, I don't owe my father any favors and after that BS last night about how women need to just settle down, be good, and make babies? No, Hayley. I'm so done with him. And nothing against my aunt – my not-mother – but I can't do this anymore. My own mother had to basically retire from modeling and move overseas so she wouldn't cause a scandal just by existing. And why? Because she and my father happened to make a baby during their affair. It's ridiculous. Let me do this."

Hayley looked around the apartment. "Um, I have no furniture. No place for you to sit. We can't really conduct an interview in my bed."

"Well, we could, but I imagine we'd get very distracted." With that announcement, Veronica leaned just inside the door and kissed Hayley. For a long, breathless moment, they shared a kiss and then Veronica stepped back and said, "You see? I'm tired of living the way I have been. I'm tired of pretending I'm not something I really am. Well, a couple of things, really. You got into journalism to tell people the truth, so tell my truth. I don't want to live in shadows anymore."

When Veronica put it like that, Hayley couldn't help but want to help her, too. "Let's go somewhere quiet," she said.

"This is quiet. I don't mind sitting on the floor. Please?"

Hayley stepped aside and opened her door wider. "Then come on in. You're my first after-college interview."

They hesitated next to the kitchen and Veronica looked at the small coffeemaker. "You really need a bigger coffee maker if you're going to be a journalist."

"I know, I know. It's a silly thing, really, but it does help me think. I'll go buy a bigger one today."

They sat cross-legged on the bed, facing each other. It seemed weirdly intimate to conduct an interview there, but as soon as Veronica started to speak, Hayley forgot their relationship. Her small handheld recorder caught every word as Veronica brought them back in time to the late 1970s and her father's affair with her mother.

"He married Patty because she was the 'stable' responsible sister," Veronica said, lifting her fingers to curl them in air quotes. "But he had an affair with Pamela because she was the hot one. My mother said she felt awful about it and she put it a stop to it when she got pregnant with me. She's the older sister and everyone pretty much adored her. My aunt Patty kind of got the short end of the stick, you know? Anyway, I was on the way, so the affair ended. Since my aunt could never seem to have kids, she and my father officially adopted me as hers."

"Wow. All his talk about how women ought to just be good girls and have children and his own wife can't? So he has a daughter with his sister-in-law? That's messed up."

"Right?" Veronica gripped her ankles and frowned. "My poor aunt Patty – she had other things going for her. Did you know she was a scientist before she married my father? He expected her to give up her job, of course. No woman of his was going to be working on engineering and physics. I think she married him because she really loved him, but it didn't turn out to be what she expected. Instead of a power couple, he systematically broke her down until she fit his mold of a perfect woman. It pisses me off that these two amazing women could have their lives ruined by this one jerk."

Hayley tried to imagine what that must have been like in the 1970s. Even now, she knew many women ended up feeling disempowered and beholden to men. "It's not fair," she finally said. "And it feels like our culture hasn't changed all that much in that regard."

"No, it hasn't. And of course it's not every man. Heck, it's not even every man in my father's generation or political party. But it's a reminder that we still have work to do. He's one of a hypocritical few who holds the power. We need to make sure people know that and realize their vote for 'family values' is actually a vote for misogynist principles that have no place in a world where human rights matter."

They both blinked at each other and then chuckled. "Are you sure you don't want to get into politics?" Hayley asked. "You'd have the women's vote."

Veronica canted her head to one side and said, "I've

considered it, but I think I'd do more harm than good. Thank you, though, for having that kind of confidence in me. It's more than I've ever had in myself."

"So what do you want to accomplish, then, in telling this story?" Hayley asked.

"To be true to myself, to encourage others to speak up, and if that means I can't stay here in Washington, that's fine. Some things are bigger than the individual. Like..." Veronica reached out and touched Hayley's face again. "Like loving you. Besides, it's not just my story. It's everyone's story."

Hayley reached up to hold Veronica's hand against her face. She was overwhelmed by her girlfriend's admissions and by the trust placed in her to make them public. That was when she realized the relationship wasn't just changing her – it was changing Veronica. It was freeing them both.

"I won't live in the shadows anymore like my mother

chose to," Veronica whispered. "Forty years have gone by and if I don't tell my story, then I'm just perpetuating a myth about a man who doesn't deserve what he has. There are better men out there. Let's celebrate them, instead of people like my father. Let's change the way things are."

This time it was Hayley who leaned in to kiss Veronica. "You're brave," she said. "Thank you for trusting me. I only hope I can do your story justice. But if I write it, what will your mother think if she reads it?"

Veronica let out a short laugh. "She'll feel vindicated. It was a weird triangle, living with my mother, father, and aunt. Mom told me the truth when I was about nine, that they were passing me off as her sister's daughter all that time. It's why they got me tutors and sent me on vacations in Europe with my mother – to hide the fact that I looked more and more like her."

That sounded unfair to Hayley, like something out of a suspense movie. How could anyone have a child and then have to keep them a secret?

"Eventually, I disappeared from the public eye, finished high school in Paris, and started modeling in Europe. But not before agreeing to keep up the charade. When people asked about my parents, I just laughed. I couldn't lie. I was too loyal to my mother, but I see now the only person who benefited from that agreement with my father. Not me, my mother, or my aunt."

"You've lived an entire life built on lies. I can't imagine what that must have been like for you or your mother, or even your aunt." Hayley bowed her head and looked at her notes. No wonder Veronica was bursting to get her story out.

She was right. It wasn't just her story.

It was the story of generations of wronged women.

And Hayley had the unique privilege of telling it.

"Are you sure?" she asked Veronica.

"Sure?" Veronica leaned forward and kissed her, threading her fingers through Hayley's long brown hair. "You're the one thing I've been sure of for the first time in a long time. I trust you with my story and I trust you with my heart. Do with both of them what you will."

As the interview turned into something far more intimate, Hayley felt herself falling even deeper in love with Veronica. The more she learned about her and understood her, the more she realized Veronica wasn't the one sweeping in to save a barista from her life of minimum wage mediocrity.

It was turning out to be the other way around.

Chapter 15

NOW THAT HAYLEY HAD a story – a real story – the words flowed. Hayley didn't know if it was because she now had a fresh angle, Veronica's perspective on her father and family, or what. But she pulled the article together in a whole new, unexpected way. It wasn't difficult to juxtapose the senator's voting record with the truth about his affair and Veronica's parentage.

No other affairs came to light in her research – it was just the one. But one was enough.

For a brief moment, Hayley felt bad about it. It seemed wrong to drag another person's life through the mud just in an effort to keep them from getting re-elected to office. Even with Veronica's reassurances that this didn't bother her, this wasn't the kind of thing Hayley ever thought of writing. It wasn't what got her excited about her work on the college newspaper. No, what got her excited was telling people about something they had no idea about and delving into what it meant for her readers. This felt a tad… slimy to her.

"But remember what he said about not condoning

gay relationships, even for 'pretty ladies'," Veronica pointed out. "If you want slimy, that's slimy. Seriously. It's creepy to talk like that. How come he gets to decide what's acceptable for women, whether he deems them pretty or not?"

Hayley used McClusky's remarks about "weakening the family unit" as a quote next to her list of very anti-family causes from whom he had accepted donations. It wasn't as startling as the assertion that he had conducted an affair with Veronica's mother. It was just the icing on the cake once the article was finished.

She finally let Veronica read the first draft over while she brewed another cup of coffee for herself. The one-cup coffeemaker was definitely due for replacement if she was going to keep drinking at this rate.

"Wow," she heard Veronica say from the bedroom. "Hayley, this is exquisite. You really are a talented writer, you know that?"

Hayley walked in there, the mug clutched between her hands, and leaned against the door. "Yeah?" she asked. "I'd pretty much started to think I lost my touch somewhere between finals and the new job."

"No, you didn't." Veronica's eyes were still focused on the laptop screen and she was smiling. "I love how you've framed it. You didn't do it in a way that calls attention to his actions, so much as point out that this is just one instance in which we show adulation for people without realizing they're basically scumbags or how we know they are, but we give them a pass for their behavior because we figure all politicians are the same. Like the next one will be just as bad or something, so it doesn't matter who we put in office."

"Those are pretty harsh words for your own father." With a sip of coffee, Hayley felt warmth flood her body. She had to admit she did feel better after writing the article. But not better in the way she hoped. She just felt good that she wrote something that exposed the truth about a person she didn't particularly like. What she wanted to feel, though, was thrilled that she had written something meaningful. This piece was far from deep or meaningful. It was a means to an end, a way to prove herself to her boss. Because that's what mattered at the moment.

"I know, but he's no better than any other famous

person who gets away with whatever they want, simply because they can. So I love that you really pinpoint that irony about a guy who preaches family values while carrying on an affair with his own sister-in-law. You nailed it, Hayley."

Nailed it. Was that what Hayley wanted to do? She sank down onto the edge of the bed and continued to drink her coffee.

"Honey, what is it?" Veronica closed the laptop and scooted over to sit behind Hayley.

"It's just that this isn't what I expected to write about. I thought I'd be telling people about things like... like GMOs in their food and stuff like that. Lifting the lid on big pharmaceutical scandals." Hayley set the coffee cup on her bedside table and shook her head. "This isn't what I had in mind. I feel like this story is too personal. I don't want it to harm you or your mother, or even your aunt."

"It won't hurt them. It will encourage them to speak up."

Hayley hated how unsure she felt. It was a huge story, one that could make or break her name as a journalist. But it was also close to her heart. Way too close.

"Aw, honey." Veronica used her hand to turn Hayley's head and pressed a kiss to her lips. "Don't worry about me. I wouldn't have told you all of this if I didn't believe you could do the story justice. You know what – let's go out and do something right now. Something fun."

"Like what?"

"I don't know, but we'll come up with something to get your mind off of this."

Hayley turned and wrapped her arms around Veronica. In just over a month, she had learned so much from this woman. It was hard to believe where they had gone in that short time. Before she knew it, Hayley's lips were on Veronica's, parting them so she could taste the inside of her mouth.

There was certainly no question of doing something fun now because Veronica responded in kind. Within moments, they were entangled in each other's arms and legs, lying on the bed as they kissed.

It was too much tension, Hayley decided. Her life

was just bursting with it. Whatever Veronica had gotten off her chest in telling the story now seemed to weigh Hayley down now instead. She had to alleviate it.

Veronica seemed to understand because she glided her hand down along Hayley's torso and beneath her shorts as they kissed. "Honey, let me help you relax," she murmured against Hayley's lips.

That was exactly what Hayley needed – help relaxing, letting go of all her doubts. Veronica's fingers worked their magic, curling and spiraling beneath her panties until Hayley shook with release.

As soon as she caught her breath, she rolled Veronica over and offered her girlfriend the same ecstasy, bringing her to orgasm with kisses and deft swirls of her fingers. They lay side by side after that, breathing heavily.

"I don't think we should stop now," Veronica said. "After all, my jeans are already on the floor. You need something more."

"More?" Hayley asked. This certainly was fun and having Veronica occupy her thoughts was far better than having anything else there. At least for the moment.

"Mmhmm." Veronica sat up and shimmied her panties off, then lifted the t-shirt over her head. "Take those shorts off, because we are done with the warm up, my dear."

Hayley pushed the loose shorts down over her hips and watched as Veronica turned around to straddle her head. Her girlfriend's hands rubbed along her legs, then parted them gently.

"Have you ever done this?" Veronica asked.

"Freshman year." Hayley's voice was a dry whisper. Her body was pulsing again, excited by the prospect of having Veronica atop her, playing with her as Hayley gave her the same pleasure in return. "I liked it a lot, but I never tried it again."

"Well, then." That lovely, dewy flesh of Veronica's was lowering closer and closer to Hayley's face. "I think it's time you really let go and enjoyed yourself today. It's been one heck of a week for us both."

Hayley thought Veronica would finally be within reach of her tongue, but instead, Veronica leaned forward and nestled her head between Hayley's legs. At the first touch of her tongue lapping at her, Hayley arched and moaned with pleasure.

"Mm, you taste so good," Veronica said. "Especially after you've come. I can't wait to make you do it again." This time when she wiggled her hips down, she finally offered herself to Hayley.

As Veronica's arms wrapped around Hayley's legs and her mouth descended again on her aching, needy pussy, Hayley licked at her girlfriend's valley. There it was, that sense of heady rapture she felt when they were close together, sharing something as intimate as sex.

Hayley wanted to be on top, but she acquiesced to lying beneath Veronica. There was something freeing about that, too. She didn't have to make any decisions because someone else was taking control. Someone else was deciding what they were doing and she was happy to go with the flow.

It was another challenge and Hayley felt her defenses fall away as they made love. Veronica wanted to be there for her, to love her and care for her. There was nothing wrong with that. In fact, the problem was that Hayley realized she loved love more than anything else in her life.

After another shared release, they showered together. Hayley relaxed under Veronica's massaging hands as her girlfriend washed her from head to toe.

"I hate how much this job stresses you out," Veronica purred as her hands rubbed up and down Hayley's back.

"Yeah. Me too." Hayley sighed and lifted her face to the stream of water. That was one good thing about her apartment – her view out the window might be other buildings, but at least everything about it was private. Like the bathroom. How funny that she ended up sharing it anyway. "It's not at all how I expected things to turn out after college."

"Right, I get you. The wide-eyed Midwestern girl came here with dreams of keeping the people informed, only to find that she's got to deal with more than just writing a news story."

"Ugh." Hayley turned around and embraced Veronica, letting the water wash the soap off her back.

Her girlfriend's chuckle vibrated through her entire body and Hayley leaned into it.

"How do you do it?" she asked.

"How do I do what?"

"Not take everything so seriously? After what you told me, I'm surprised you're in such good humor."

"Oh, sweetie." Veronica's hands caressed her back, chasing the bubbles away, and then she turned off the shower. "I realized that if I cared too much, I would go crazy. My mom taught me that. Maybe I also benefitted from all those years I spent in Paris. I learned to have the French outlook on life. Live it and don't let it get me down too much."

Hayley reached for one of the fluffy towels on the rack next to the shower and offered it to Veronica, before reaching around to take the other. "I wish I could let stuff just roll off my back like that," she muttered.

"I'm sure you could if you tried, but it takes years of practice. Years. Living on nothing but coffee and cigarettes when you're a teenager helps a little bit, but I'm not sure I would love you if you were just like me."

"Why is that?" Hayley squinted at Veronica and then scrubbed her towel over her face.

"Well, what I love about you are all the qualities I lack or the qualities I have, but subsume. Like the

control issue. You want to be in control. So do I, but I
hide it well by batting my eyelashes and playing games."
Veronica held her towel to her chest and struck a pose,
then fluttered her eyelashes.

It was funny, yes, but Hayley also knew it was
painfully true. Veronica's skills all had to do with hiding
her true self, just so she could live her life the way she
wanted. It sounded like an oxymoron, yet she understood
it. Even though she'd never quite had to hide who she
was, she couldn't exactly flaunt it back home.

"This isn't what I want," Hayley said at last, "for
either of us. I want…" She blew out a breath and
lowered her towel as she rolled her gaze toward the
ceiling. "I want to write about things that matter, without
worrying about who I might hurt in the process."

"Then you do not want to be a journalist," Veronica
said. "You picked the wrong profession. You like giving
to people. Maybe that's what you should be doing."

"I don't think that's the case. I just think maybe I
chose the wrong employer. Or the wrong city. It was
naïve of me to just take the first job offer when I
probably could have done so much better. I graduated

summa cum laude, for goodness sake."

Veronica stepped forward to hug her. "You did and I bet if you don't limit yourself to just one city, you'll find that there are lots of people who want you. Give it a shot. Washington isn't the only place where you can get the big scoops."

"That's beautiful and…" Hayley stuck out her tongue. "Incredibly sappy."

"Yeah, well, that's how I roll. Get used to it." Veronica tightened her hug. "Tell you what – let's go buy that coffee maker and after that, I'll give you the free time you need to sort stuff out. Does that sound good?"

Hayley nodded. It did sound good. But what sounded better was the idea of visiting home. She had promised her sister, after all. Could she, though? It had only been a week since graduation. Not only that but one week into her new job. The odds of getting vacation time were low. As appealing as it sounded, running away wasn't a solution.

The problem was, she didn't know how to solve the problems she had.

Chapter 16

Hayley held her breath as Jill read the article, the editor's narrowed eyes flicking back and forth as she looked at the screen. When she was done, she looked at Hayley over her monitor. Those merciless eyes were narrowed, lips pressed into a thin line, and cheeks sucked in.

"Where's your proof? You've made some wild claims here, so where is your proof of them?" Jill asked. "Birth certificates, hospital records, DNA. If blood is what it takes, then I want blood, Becker."

Hayley's heart thumped in her chest. "It's a first-hand account," she said. "Any records… Well, they could have been tampered with in some way. We have the daughter's word and the mother's word on it."

"No, we have a case of she said, she said, and you know he'll deny it. That's the thing politicians do best. Without proof, you're going to get the Feminist Flag sued for libel and slander. Don't fuck with this kind of story. Don't you remember anything you learned about journalism?" Jill pinched the bridge of her nose and said,

"God, how you managed to graduate with honors is beyond me. Stick with what you know, Becker – your wide-eyed middle America white bread perspective. I'm assigning this to someone else, someone who will give me a clean story and do their research."

It was the worst kind of dismissal, just short of a firing. Hayley left Jill's office, trudged to her desk, and sank down into her chair. Everything about this job was setting her up for failure. Everything. At a legitimate newspaper, she would have had a mentor, someone invested in her success to guide and train her. Here, she had Jill. And she felt incredibly defeated. Only a week in and she wanted to be anywhere but here.

It was the first time she'd ever really wanted to throw in the towel, to call it quits. What had happened to the strong girl who gave, gave, gave to everyone around her?

She didn't belong here, though. Working at the *Feminist Flag* didn't align at all with her ambitions. Why had she compromised her values like that?

"And why am I whining?" she muttered to herself, dropping her head onto her arms. "She doesn't owe me anything regardless of whether or not I graduated with honors. Nobody owes me anything. She's right – I'm forgetting basic things I should know by now."

"Uh, Hayley, who are you talking to?"

Hayley jerked upright and looked at Elise, who stood over her desk with two take-out coffee cups clutched in her hands. "Myself, apparently."

"Oh no. What happened? Was it her again?"

"Who else? It was my article on McClusky. She hated it, questioned my abilities as a journalist, and decided to reassign it. She was right, though. I really messed up."

Hayley was glad she didn't have to specify who "she" was. At this point, both she and Elise had learned that nearly everyone else in the office also treaded lightly around their editor, sometimes referring to her as "she who will not be named."

"I don't know what I was thinking. I was… Ugh." Hayley pulled several tissues from the box on her desk and blotted at her eyes. "I was blinded by my feelings for Veronica. I wanted to do right by her, so I thought taking the assignment was the only way. Anyone else won't write with an ounce of sensitivity. They'll just slay McClusky with words, whether he deserves it or not."

"Wow." Elise stared at her. "That's the most I've heard you speak all in one go. This is serious, chatty lady."

"So serious, that I think I just want to go home."

"Aw, honey." Now Elise perched on the edge of the desk and looked down at her. "Running away isn't the answer. It might give you some perspective, but it won't fix anything. You need to take some time to think, though. Maybe jumping into a job like this right out of school wasn't the best idea."

Hayley shook her head so hard, she made herself dizzy. "I think all the damn time. I analyze and over-analyze, and then analyze my analysis. Maybe thinking is the last thing I need to do. Maybe I need to just go with my instincts. As long as I'm with Veronica, I can't work in D.C. I just can't. There's no way for me to be objective. Everything I write will be affected by our relationship unless I can find another job. Being a barista was easier than this. I'd rather serve coffee again than deal with all of this conflict."

With a tilt of her head, Elise said, "Whoa, hold up. First of all, you don't mean that. The last thing you want to do is go back to making coffee for people with more disposable income than you. Second, far be it for me to tell you what to do with your life. It sounds like you've figured it out. Are you going to quit?"

"Not yet. I'm going to talk to Veronica first and tell her how I feel. In the meantime..." Hayley slid her gaze to her computer and grinned. "I'm going to finish that article. Since Jill is reassigning it, my work is still mine. I just hope she doesn't tell the next writer to follow-up on what I presented. I want to break this story first, if ever."

"You're not serious." Elise shifted away from the desk as Hayley rose to her feet and started shoving her belongings into her purse.

"I'm totally serious. Like I said, I would rather go back to being a barista than putting up with this crap. And you're right – I need time to think." Hayley draped the shoulder strap over her right arm and gripped the back of the chair. "Look, Veronica trusted me with her story. If anyone is going to put it out there, it's me. I'm just going to spend the rest of my day making my claim to it."

Elise returned her grin and offered her one of the coffee cups. "Then you're going to need this."

Hayley held it up. "Thank you, Elise." She turned and walked out of the office. As soon as she was in the elevator, she sent Veronica a text message. By the time she reached the first floor, she had her reply. Her smile only grew as she strode out of the building and hailed a taxi.

To her delight, Veronica met her at the hospital. She looked beautiful in her khaki slacks and teal button-down shirt. Beautiful and perplexed. Hayley wanted to kiss those quirked lips then and there, but she simply hugged Veronica and said, "Thank you for meeting me here."

"You're welcome, but why did you need to know where I was born?" Veronica asked as they walked into the building.

"Because I need to verify every single aspect of the story you gave me. I'm going to prove I'm a serious journalist and that I know what I'm doing. Tell me about your birth certificate. Was I right about what it says?"

"You mean that piece of paper that lists Patty as my mother, instead of Pamela? My father's got deep pockets and connections willing to do anything his way. The birth certificate is proof of that."

Hayley clenched her fists. "I knew it. I just knew it."

"So if my father was able to get the public record altered, despite the very obvious fact that I came out of Pamela's vagina, what is the point of a visit to the hospital?"

"Because the medical records will show that it was Pamela Stone admitted to the maternity ward, not Patricia McClusky. And since you're the child, you are going to ask for access. Most records are sealed unless you're the subject of the record. Considering you're the child who was born, you're one of the subjects." Hayley looked at Veronica and then reached out to take her hand. "That is, if you're willing to help me. If you want this story told, we're going to tell it. Not anyone else. It's not their right."

Veronica smiled as she accepted Hayley's hand.

"Thank you. You know, I've never seen you look so determined since I've known you. I like this side of you. It's adorable and I've been waiting for it to come out."

"Good." Hayley turned her gaze forward again and they approached the medical records office.

Just as Hayley hoped, Veronica sweet-talked her way into getting the records of her birth without even dropping her father's name. Soon Veronica handed over the fee and the clerk handed them a sealed envelope with the records. Both women walked out of the building, giddy with triumph.

Veronica didn't pull the papers out until they were sitting in the backseat of her car. She even put up the dark tinted window that separated the front seat from the back. "My mother told me about this, but it's still weird to have the records in my hands," she said, letting out a breath as she held the open envelope in both hands. "I shouldn't look, though. You should. It was your idea. You're the one who really gets the satisfaction in the end, so go for it."

Hayley only hesitated for a moment before taking the large envelope from Veronica and sliding the records out

of it. On the first of several pages, she had her proof.
"Pamela Stone," she whispered, "and a baby girl born on
April 29, 1977. Gosh, I didn't know you just had a
birthday. I wish you'd told me."

When she looked up, Veronica was blowing out a
breath and flicking the window control. "I didn't think
about it. Even without my father's name, I'm so
privileged, you know. Because of my mother being who
she was in the 1960s and 1970s. When I think about it, I
realize that would have been good enough for me all this
time – just to be my mother's daughter and have nothing
to do with my father, you know?"

The way she turned and covered her face with her
hand made Hayley's heart skip a beat. This was
supposed to be their moment, but instead, Veronica was
sagging as if exhausted. The feeling was entirely mutual.

"What is it?" she asked.

"It's that…" Veronica blew out a breath and turned
to her. "It doesn't matter anymore. That's what it is. It
never really mattered, now that I think about it. And I
can't do this. Heck, I can't stay here in D.C. anymore.
I'm tired of it, Hayley. So tired of it. I've been longing to

get away from all of this and to get back to being exactly that – just my mother's daughter. No connection to my father anymore."

"Running away isn't the answer." Hayley found herself repeating Elise's earlier words to her, but they rang hollow. She could tell Veronica's mind was already made up, her intention set.

"Neither is staying here and subjecting myself to a life I'm so tired of living. Hayley, I'm forty-years-old. Forty. I'm a grown woman and the sacrifices I make for appearances are bullshit. I won't apologize anymore. I won't live like this, treading a fine line between decorum and authenticity."

She was right and Hayley bowed her head. "I know what you mean. I can't do it either."

"Can't do what?" Veronica sounded panicked. "This? Us? What do you mean?"

"No." Hayley looked at her again. "No. I can't do this as in be with you and have this job. I have to make a choice."

Veronica went pale beneath her make-up and fear radiated from her, fear that Hayley had to assuage.

"I choose you." She reached out to clasp Veronica's hands between hers. "D.C. isn't the place for us if we want to be together. You're right. We need to figure out what matters most. When I got into journalism, it was because I believed in the integrity of the press. I still do, but maybe being a staff writer isn't what I wanted all this time. But I don't want to think about it anymore. My first priority is loving you. You have taught me to get back to the heart of what matters to me."

"Loving you matters most to me." Veronica's lips met hers in a wild, passionate kiss, reminiscent of that first, unexpected intimate encounter. Their hands tangled in each other's hair and even though Hayley was aware of the driver in the front seat, separated from them by nothing more than a pane of tinted glass, she couldn't stop herself.

It was the first choice she'd made in the past two weeks that felt right – love first. The rest no longer mattered.

"Wait. Okay." Veronica ended the kiss, breathing heavily, her eyes lidded. "We need to think logically. You have a lot of money saved up, right?"

"I do," Hayley acknowledged, still dazzled by the kiss. Veronica wanted to go from kissing to discussing money? "Why?"

"Because you won't need it. Leave it in the bank. Save it for later, for when we need to settle down."

"What are we going to do, then?"

Veronica let out a little laugh. "What lovers ought to do in the spring – we're going to Paris."

Chapter 17

"AND THEN I SAID, 'I'm not sure I'm cut out for this job or the ethical implications of the articles you assign us to write. And she said," Hayley cleared her throat and pitched her voice slightly lower, "'Well, then, run along back to the coffee shop, girl'."

"Oh, oh my gosh." Veronica clapped her hands together with glee and shook her head. "What a bitch!"

"Yup." Hayley put her hands on her hips and stared at the suitcases as Veronica's driver put them in the backseat of the car. "Even with her insult, whatever. I'm done."

At first, Hayley was worried quitting meant she lacked strength, but now she felt like it meant the opposite. Asserting herself and putting her wishes first made her feel stronger than ever. For once it wasn't about what was logical or right for someone else, like her parents or another authority figure. It was about her and what she really wanted in the moment.

The driver closed the trunk and held the door open for the ladies. It was still strange to Hayley to be treated this way, to slide inside Veronica's plush vehicle and settle in without another thought. She looked out the window at the apartment building and sighed. Veronica had helped her get out of the lease. It did cost her deposit, but Hayley was able to let that go.

In fact, for the first time, she was able to let many things go.

She felt her breath quicken as she opened her purse and checked the contents. There it was – her passport. She applied for one during her first year of college in the hopes of maybe going overseas, but it never happened. Still, it was money well spent for ten years of possibilities.

Now it represented a possibility about to be fulfilled. How had she gone from recent college graduate to being swept off her feet and taken to Paris? Hayley didn't know, but she knew she had to do it. All those years of hard work – it was time to play.

"Hey, is this going to be a *Say Anything* moment?" Veronica asked.

"Huh?"

The blonde laughed. "Don't tell me you've never

seen it."

"Never seen it," Hayley confirmed.

"Okay, so I don't want to spoil it, but one of the characters wants to fly to Paris, but she's scared of flying. Do you need someone to fly with you or are you fine on airplanes?"

"No, totally fine. Though I've never gone overseas, so this should be interesting."

And it was. By the time they were on a non-stop one-way flight to Paris, Hayley felt strangely free. Untethered from everything she was leaving further and further behind her.

Until.

"Oh, crap!" Hayley fumbled in her purse for her phone.

"What is it?" Veronica asked, her brow creased with concern.

"Um, everything was so spontaneous and we were so busy over the past couple of days, I forgot to tell my family about it."

"Whoa, hold on." Veronica reached out and placed her hand over Hayley's. "First of all, take a deep breath and relax. You can inform them when we land. Second, how could you forget something like that? I mean, I didn't tell my father and non-mother, but I have reasons for that."

"Right. Of course." Hayley held her phone up, squinted at it, then laid it on the tray table and closed her eyes. "It's just that we had to make arrangements, pack, I had to get everything into storage… How could I forget to at least call them?"

Veronica turned completely sideways in her roomy first-class seat and propped her elbow up on it as she regarded Hayley. "First of all, don't come unglued on me now. You've finally learned to let go of control. Take a breath. Everything is fixable."

"Okay. What's your second point?"

To her surprise, Veronica shrugged. "I don't have one. But go with the first and you'll be just fine."

Hayley relaxed back in her seat and stared ahead. "I'm sorry. Considering I was so gung-ho to do this, you're right. I need to let go."

"Trust me, that's a lesson we both need to learn." Veronica turned and played with the control that made the seat recline. "Ha, I love these things. You can lay so far back in first class. Hey." She lowered her voice to a whisper. "Hayley."

"What?" Hayley rolled her head around to look at Veronica.

"Let's join the Mile High Club."

The suggestion made Hayley snort and she sat upright to cover her face with her hands. "You can't be serious."

"I'm very serious, but I understand if you're not ready." Veronica wriggled a bit in the seat, looking as if she were getting comfortable. "Just let me know if you change your mind. I'll be here."

Hayley reclined and looked at Veronica again. Somehow, the blonde seemed to be sleeping, eyes closed, lashes dark against her skin. She looked like she would be comfortable in Paris, like striding through the most fashionable neighborhoods would come effortlessly to her.

Could Hayley free herself in that way? Could she cultivate that certain je ne sais quoi? Was she even making the right choice now?

"I can feel you analyzing again," Veronica muttered without opening her eyes.

"What? No."

"Yes." Veronica opened one eye and glared at her. "Stop doing that. Think about what Hayley wants and then let's focus on making sure Hayley gets what Hayley wants."

Hayley narrowed her eyes. "You just said that so you could say my name three times in one sentence."

"I like saying your name. Give me time to catch a catnap and we'll find reasons to say each other's names again and again once we're at my place."

Veronica sounded so relaxed, so casual. She had *a place* in Paris. It felt strange to think she would be staying with Veronica at her place, her Paris apartment. She realized she had to stop analyzing, just like Veronica said. This was something for her to just enjoy. It was a chance to reevaluate her life and rediscover herself.

Finally, Hayley lay back in her seat and closed her own eyes. What would it take to sort out her life? She didn't know. She imagined Veronica had answers that involved topless sunbathing on the Riviera.

Fortunately, when they landed Veronica didn't mention anything about being topless or saying each other's names. In fluent French, she procured assistance in getting their luggage and finding a car. The entire airport experience went by in a whirlwind. Hayley didn't even commit anything she heard or saw to memory because she was overwhelmed by the strangeness of everything around her.

When they walked into Veronica's apartment, Hayley finally took a deep breath and stood just inside the door. The driver left after helping with the luggage and shut the door behind him. Veronica turned and stared at her in silence, waiting.

"Wow," Hayley finally said. She crossed the apartment and looked out the window. "Wow," she repeated. "You and your views. They're an international thing."

"Hey, are you going to be okay?" Veronica asked, taking a step toward her.

Hayley looked around the apartment. It was a pristine, white space with a quaint charm to it. And, of course, an amazing view of the city.

"The Eiffel Tower," Hayley said, pointing out the large window.

"Yeah, that's what you're seeing. You'll see it all lit up at night, too. Some people hate it, some people love it. It's grown on me."

Hayley finally walked forward and sank down onto the large, white wraparound sofa. "I can't believe I'm here. Everything was... it was all laid out for me. I mean, I laid it out eight years ago. Sure, I was only a freshman in high school, but I thought I had it figured out, you know? I worked my ass off academically and in part time jobs to get to college, to save up all that money so I could get a start in life. I didn't want to rely on my parents for anything because they work so hard for so little. And now I'm here."

Unconsciously, she rubbed her hand over the buttery smooth fabric of the sofa. It was, of course, wonderful to touch. Like Veronica.

"Now I'm here," she repeated, "and I'm realizing every plan I made doesn't feel right anymore. Do you know what I mean?"

"Sweetie." Veronica sat next to her and angled her

body so their knees were touching. "I understand more than anybody else could. I had the same plans, you know. Well, not the same, but when I was in high school, I knew exactly what I wanted. I wanted to be just like my mother. So I did it. I modeled for sixteen years and then I turned thirty and realized it was fun, but it wasn't fulfilling. I was accumulating things, but nothing meaningful. So that's when I started to pay more attention to what my father did and I didn't like what I saw there."

Hayley leaned into her girlfriend's touch as Veronica's hand went to her hair, stroking it. "So what did you do?"

"That's when I started using my money and my name for things that mattered. I'm really proud of the difference I've been able to make for the past ten years, but at what price? I still can't live out as myself. Not fully and completely. That needs to change. I can do more for people. I realize that now. And I have something in mind, but first I want to see what you need."

"What I need?" Reaching up to hold Veronica's hand

against her face, Hayley lifted her gaze.

"Yes. Like I said, I know what I want. So now I need to know what you want. Well, *you* need to know what you want, and I'll do what I can to help."

Tears pricked at Hayley's eyes. "I need to know what I want, too. How am I going to figure it out?"

"Oh, sweetie." Veronica leaned closer and pulled her into a warm embrace. "I don't know, but I think the best thing to do is strip away everything from the past month, maybe even the past year, and then get to the heart of the matter. Go back to a simpler time and what inspired you in the first place. If you do that, you might have your answer."

They exchanged kisses that were wet and salty tasting. Hayley wished she could staunch the flow of tears, but she couldn't. They seemed to want to come no matter what. It hardly mattered, though, because Veronica was there with her. She matched her kiss for kiss, caress for caress until they were making love on that supple sofa.

It seemed strange to be lying there naked, entangled in each other's arms when they were done. Hayley tried to rise up, but Veronica said, "Don't mind the sofa. I'm just happy we're here together."

"I know, but what if..."

"What if what? We're alone here. No one is going to walk in on us if that's what you're worried about." Veronica sat up and pushed her hair back away from her face. "I guess it's another thing you need to learn to let go of – this belief that everything must be done conventionally. You're a lesbian, so you're already unconventional according to some definitions of the word."

"Yeah, I suppose so." Hayley blinked up at her and said, "What next, then?"

"Well..." Veronica's gaze strayed around the apartment and then she laughed. "We're going to get it on in every room in this apartment. I think that will alleviate your need to do everything the so-called 'right' way."

Hayley finally lifted herself up on her elbows and smirked. "Like you said, I'm a lesbian. At least part of me decided the unconventional way is the right way."

"That's a start then, isn't it?" Veronica smiled and

kissed her. "Let's just see if we can get the rest of you to get on the unconventional ship and work your way through this mindset of yours."

"What do you think it's from?" Hayley asked, watching as Veronica started plucking clothes off the floor.

"What? Your mindset?" Veronica handed her a bra and t-shirt. "If you're asking me to psychoanalyze you, I have to admit that's outside my realm of ability."

Hayley thrust her arms into her bra and clasped the front of it between her breasts. "Not exactly, but you seem to be able to get to the heart of everything about me. Why am I the way I am? Why can't I just relax and go with the flow, and why did I settle for a job I never wanted in the first place."

"This is a pretty deep conversation for naked time, but here's my take on it." Veronica also put on her bra, then turned it around to wiggle it into place. "First of all, your parents – they work hard and have very little. You don't want to be like them or rely on them for anything. You feel like a burden to them in a way, so you needed to make it on your own. As for the job, you didn't want to be a graduate stuck at a coffee shop. Getting a job was highly competitive and you were frustrated that you couldn't keep up with your peers, so you accepted the offer you got, even though it wasn't what you wanted. How did I do?"

"Great. Now tell me, is there anything I did right since graduation?"

Veronica leaned into her and gave her a cocky grin. "Me," she answered.

Chapter 18

AFTER A FEW NIGHTS in Paris, they went to a chic restaurant to meet Veronica's mother.

Hayley was having more fun in Paris than she'd ever had in her life. She felt that, in a way, it wasn't fair. She should be back in D.C. trying harder at her job, or in Nebraska visiting her parents. Veronica was probably getting tired of hearing her fret about work and family.

It was as they sat down to dinner that Veronica said, "You know, the whole reason we're here is to learn to let go of the 'I think I should' and instead focus on the 'I know I want.' Your entire life has been an 'I think I should,' my dear type A."

Hayley grimaced and looked down at the napkin and utensils in front of her.

"Don't get me wrong – I love you just the way you are," Veronica added, "but we're here because both of us realized our lives were going in the wrong direction."

"Pity," came an unfamiliar voice. "I thought you were here to see me."

"Oh, that too, Mother." Veronica rose from her chair

and hugged the woman who stood behind her.

With a few blinks, Hayley adjusted her focus and realized Pamela Stone was even more stunning in real life than in photos. It was obvious that Veronica had inherited her looks from this woman with her delicate, dark eyebrows and buttery blonde hair. Of course, Pamela had a few facial lines here and there, as one might expect for a woman in her sixties. But those lines, Hayley decided, made her even more beautiful.

For a brief, tummy-flipping moment, she thought about her own mother. Yes, those lines represented years of experiences, and those experiences made women like her mother and Veronica's mother strong. They weren't beautiful in spite of it. They were beautiful because of it.

"Mother, I would like to introduce you to someone special," Veronica announced, turning toward Hayley. "This is Hayley Becker, my girlfriend. Hayley, this is my mother, Pamela Stone. Do not confuse her with the Rolling Stones. Yes, she hung out with them, and no, she did not inspire their name."

"Ah, Hayley. Enchante." Even with her American origins, Pamela managed a decent French accent. Better than anything Hayley could fake. She supposed years of living in Paris helped with nailing down proper inflection.

"Wow, it's incredible to meet you," Hayley said, rising to her feet and offering her hand.

"You know that's not how they do it in France." Pamela stepped around the table and gave Hayley a kiss on each cheek. "There you go. It's one of the customs I love here. I think it keeps things more civilized." Her voice had a slightly husky quality to it, from age, Hayley figured.

She realized as they sat at the table that she was sitting with a woman who had seen it all – the turmoil of the 1960s and 1970s that had shaped her country. Hayley could not fight the awe rising inside her. This was the kind of thing that had inspired her when she was younger – people like Pamela Stone who had experiences someone two generations younger could only dream of.

It was people, Hayley realized, not just news that mattered to her. "I… I feel like I'm going to fangirl," she said, "yet I didn't even know who you were until I met

Veronica. But now I feel like…"

"Like you're seeing living history? I know."

Veronica had a wide grin on her face. It wasn't one of her practiced, charming ones, but a truly deep smile that emphasized her laugh lines. "Trust me, it even blows my mind that this woman hung with people like Jagger and Warhol, maybe even the Beatles."

Pamela lifted her hand and said, "That's enough about me. Everything you want to know is on the internet these days. Tell me about you two."

Hayley glanced at Veronica, who looked back at her. That smile softened and Hayley's heart leaped. "What is there to tell?" Veronica asked, her voice also softer. "This is the woman I love, Mother, and I am happy for you to finally meet her."

The server approached their table and Pamela fired off an order in rapid, fluent French. Hayley just nodded when Pamela gestured around the table and the waiter gave a short affirmation before walking away.

"Don't worry. You'll like dinner," Veronica told Hayley.

"I trust your mother." It seemed like the right thing

241

to say, even though Hayley still didn't know the woman.

"So my daughter tells me you've been in Paris for a few days. How long are you staying?" Pamela asked.

Hayley and Veronica exchanged glances. "I think that's still up for debate," Hayley said slowly.

"Yeah," Veronica agreed as they both stared at each other. "But…"

"I miss…" Hayley felt a goofy grin on her face. "I miss my family and Nebraska."

"So we won't be staying too long," Veronica affirmed, looking back at her mother. "But we aren't going back to Washington, either."

"Good. Good. I never approved of you living there. Not my place to tell you what to do with your life, of course, but you're too vibrant to get mired in that dirty water." Pamela nodded and looked at the ashtray in the middle of the table. "Sometimes I wish I still smoked, but I gave it up in the 80s. Do you smoke, Hayley?"

What kind of question was that? "No, I don't."

"I'm not surprised. I think Millennials tend to be healthier than we were. But there's something to be said for having a vice. Just one guilty pleasure that doesn't harm you."

That was interesting to hear from someone's parent and Hayley felt herself liking Pamela. It was like talking to a wise aunt or older sister. "Um, I guess Veronica is my vice."

"Tell me about it." Pamela looked up at the waiter and thanked him for serving the wine, then lifted her glass. "Mm, this is my favorite. Try it."

Hayley wasn't much of a drinker, but she tried the wine and then grimaced. The wine wasn't like the fruity white zinfandel she liked to have once in a while. It was dark, almost smoky in flavor.

"Mother's tastes aren't for everyone," Veronica said. "I'll drink yours."

"Thanks." Hayley slid her wineglass to Veronica and looked at Pamela again. "And I guess what I mean about Veronica is that she made me look outside of myself. Not in a bad way, but in a way I'd never considered before."

The way Veronica's mother smiled reminded Hayley so much of her beautiful girlfriend. "That's good," Pamela said. "It's good that you recognize that and support each other in that way. That is what someone who loves you should do – help you grow and learn. I envy that. I had it once, you know."

Veronica rested her chin on her palm and smiled at her mother. "Oh, do tell, Mother."

Pamela let out a light laugh. "Well, it wasn't your father, obviously. It was someone with a heck of a lot more charm. There's no denying the Brits have plenty of it."

"Was it Mick Jagger?" Hayley couldn't help but ask, considering people couldn't seem to mention Pamela without mentioning him too.

The next laugh was throatier, deeper. "No. He was a good friend, but that was it. The point is, I found someone who was true to me and also urged me to be true to myself. That's what matters, ladies. Remember that. Now, tell me about your plans after Paris."

Hayley was impressed by Pamela's timing because the waiter served their food as she spoke. The question rolled around in her mind, though, and she stared at her food, not sure how to answer it. What were they going to do after Paris? Where was she going? What were her goals?

"I think our plans are still fluid," Veronica said, meeting Hayley's gaze. "Both of us agreed we needed to get out of D.C., but we haven't looked beyond that. Our time here is kind of like hitting the reset button."

"Mmhm," Pamela murmured as she swallowed a bite of her meal. After dabbing at her mouth with the cloth napkin, she said, "You're overdue for the reset, Veronica. I'm not surprised. And Hayley, well, considering you recently graduated from college, I'm not surprised about you either."

"Why is that?" Hayley asked. She was truly intrigued. This wasn't the kind of thing she ever discussed with her mother or younger sister. Life was very straightforward, as far as everyone in her family was concerned. You figured out what you wanted to do and then you did it. Never once had she questioned her own plans.

Pamela sipped at her wine and then picked up her fork again. "There come several moments in our lives when we re-evaluate. It happens for many college graduates when they step out into the real world or as graduation is looming, and they realize they don't know what to expect in the leap from academia to career. It's hard. Even the most accomplished student with a set life path finds it difficult. That's not a bad thing. It's natural. As for my lovely daughter…"

"Yes, Mother?" Veronica took a bite of her juicy, red steak, and then offered a piece to Hayley. "I sit here ready to learn from your years of wisdom."

"I know you do." They exchanged smirks, the kind of expressions that indicated a deep mother-daughter bond. "You hit your first rethinking point around twenty-two or so like Hayley is now, but none other since then. Now, around twenty-eight, most women get very confident and feel like they've figured it all out. But then by the time we're thirty-five or so, it all falls apart. It's like a weird, personal seven-year-itch."

"By the way," Veronica said, turning to Hayley, "I forgot to tell you my mother has women's lives worked out on a timetable. Don't delve too deeply into it – I've never understood it. Numerology or some woo-woo shit…"

"Hey." Pamela pointed, her index finger moving

back and forth between them. "Don't knock the woo-woo shit, ladies. It's pertinent. Hayley, don't let Veronica give you her 'I'm so cynical' act. I taught her better than that."

Somehow over the course of dinner, the conversation wove around and around again, back to their relationship. It flowed seamlessly and all three women ended up slightly giddy on wine and girl talk. Until Pamela asked a bigger question than any of her previous ones.

"So, where do you both see this going?"

Hayley's mouth dropped open and she turned to Veronica, who mirrored her expression. Then Hayley couldn't help it. She giggled. The laugh bubbled up before she could stop it and she clamped her hand over her mouth.

"What's funny?" Veronica asked, her smile faltering just a bit.

"It's another question we don't have the answer to. It's just..." Hayley shrugged. "We don't have the answers to anything, do we? You and I, we're like these random ships without compasses. Or maps. Or something."

"Or something." Veronica lowered her gaze, her voice softer. "Is that a problem?"

"No. Maybe. I... I haven't figured it out yet." Whether it was the food or the white wine she had ordered for herself, Hayley didn't know. But something was churning in her mind.

Veronica. She was the one thing Hayley never planned for and now she was the one thing throwing a monkey wrench in those carefully-cultivated, pre-existing plans.

Maybe it wasn't Washington she needed to get away from. Maybe it was... Veronica?

The thought made her heart lurch.

Life before Veronica had been boring. *Boring as fuck.*

"Excuse me?"

Hayley looked up and realized both Veronica and Pamela were staring at her. "What?" she asked.

"You said 'boring as fuck'," Veronica pointed out. "I feel like I'm missing something."

"No. You're not the one missing anything. I am. Or I

was before you." Hayley looked at Pamela. "Ms. Stone, you asked where we see this going. I don't know about Veronica, but I see this as a permanent thing."

"Hay…" Veronica blinked and held her hand up.

"No, Veronica. Listen to me. You changed my life big time. I don't care if leaving every stupid plan behind means I spend the rest of my life serving coffee. That's okay with me as long as you're there."

She reached over to hold Veronica's hand and felt her breath catch when Veronica laced her fingers with hers.

"I'm glad you said that, because I've had a kind of weird idea on my mind lately," Veronica said haltingly. "If you'll bear with me, I'd like to tell you about it."

Chapter 19

"WOW, THIS INTERVIEW TURNED out great." Hayley held up the magazine and said, "Listen to this: 'I simply do not want to be part of the political life. All I've wanted to do is separate myself from my father's work and reputation, something I've been striving to do behind the scenes for a long time now. But I've accepted that I need to do it more publicly. It's just that I've been afraid until now.' Jeez, Veronica, this is gold."

Veronica laughed and finished fastening her hair up at the back of her head. "I know. I've spent enough years in the public eye to know what they want to hear. But it was the first time I got to say what was in my heart." She turned and tilted her head a bit. "How do I look?"

"Gorgeous, of course. That's why you're the face of the entire project." Even though she loved her girlfriend, Hayley couldn't help but feel a little envious of her model-perfect beauty. It was their last day in Paris after almost two months there and Veronica managed to look like she belonged on a runway, even for a simple last hurrah shopping trip. Of course, the pictures of her alongside the article in one of the most renowned international magazines were also perfection. How the magazine had tracked Veronica down in Paris just to ask why she hadn't been seen in D.C. since the end of May, Hayley didn't know. But it had been an interesting encounter.

Veronica turned back to the mirror and applied her usual red lipstick. "I don't think the project needs a face, really. Especially not mine. Do you?"

"Well, you did tell the interviewer you have an amazing endeavor you can't wait to unveil. What are you going to show people? A handful of coffee beans?"

"No." Veronica finished her lipstick and then turned to grasp Hayley's hand. "I'm going to show them you."

"What's that supposed to – whoa!" Hayley yelped as Veronica yanked her off the bed and toward the door. "Wait, my purse."

Veronica scoffed and opened the door. "You don't need it."

"Yeah, I do. We're going shopping, remember?"

"No more shopping. We're going to the stylist."

Hayley knew Veronica meant what she said when

she got the urge to do something. There was nothing to do but follow along and hope for the best outcome.

Before Hayley could completely process what was happening, they were in a salon not far from the apartment and Veronica was speaking to a stylist in rapid French. And then the stylist was behind Hayley saying, "I'm just going to give it a bit of shape, okay?"

Somehow Hayley relaxed into the man's capable hands. It might have been the glass of champagne and platter of fruit that helped. Or it could have been the array of perfumed scents and low, French voices around her that lulled her into a serene state. Then, of course, there was the hair washing and deep conditioning treatment. Whatever it was, Hayley gave herself over to it and waited for whatever transformation Veronica had put into motion.

When the stylist, an assistant, and Veronica gathered around her chair an hour later, Hayley asked, "Well, how did it go? Do I look like a fashionable Parisian now?"

"See for yourself." Veronica stepped forward and spun the chair so Hayley could see her reflection in the large mirror.

Even though she was prepared for a huge transformation, Hayley did a double take when she realized she looked…

…exactly the same.

But, no, not exactly the same. She had bangs now and the ends of her hair were cut at an angle that brushed over her shoulders with each turn of her head. The length was only a bit shorter, but it had a more modern look to it.

"Wow, this is not what I expected," Hayley said, turning and tilting her head from side to side, and watching how her hair moved.

"What did you think was going to happen – some kind of radical hair style from a 1980s music video or dystopian science-fiction movie?" Veronica asked with a laugh.

"No. I just expected something… different." Hayley reached up and found that her hair was even softer to the touch now, thanks to the conditioning treatment. "This is gorgeous," she said. "Thank you."

Veronica was still grinning at her in a way that was almost maddening, like she had something up her sleeve.

"I know that look," Hayley said, spinning to face her. "Spill the beans."

"Ah, that's an appropriate pun, considering what I have in mind. Your new look is exactly what we need for the shop."

Rising from the chair, Hayley narrowed her eyes and folded her arms. "Veronica..." Even with her decision to drop everything and leave D.C., to fly off to Europe with her girlfriend nearly two months ago, she still wasn't fond of surprises.

"Yes, sweetie? Do you want to know what I'm thinking?" Veronica stepped forward and grasped Hayley's shoulders, keeping her gaze level. "I think you, dearest, are going to be the face of our new project. Not me – you, the beautiful, wide-eyed Midwestern girl who represents hard work, an open mind and, above all else, love."

"I don't know about that. I'm not a model – you are. Put me in front of a camera and I won't know what to do."

"Don't worry. I don't mean you alone. If we do this together..." Veronica turned so her arm was draped across Hayley's shoulders and they looked at themselves in the mirror. "Together we represent love and that's what this project is all about – love. I don't want to be posing on some poster or website, smiling all by myself, trying to represent the gay community. That's pointless. I want to be there with you. We're partners in all ways. Let's make sure the world knows it."

And that, Hayley realized, was why it was time for them to go back home. They had figured out exactly what they needed to learn here. All along, it was never fame or fortune for Hayley. It wasn't even prestige that mattered. It was just doing something meaningful which, for her, was telling people the truth about what was happening in their world.

Now, though, they had another way of sharing truth – another idea for how they could shape the world through it.

"Are you sure?" she asked Veronica. "We decided it would be you because people know you. They recognize you and would be more likely to pay attention."

"I'm completely sure," Veronica answered as they walked to the cash register and she paid for the visit. "If you don't mind putting our relationship out there, this is exactly what we need to do. Our brand needs to be an authentic reflection of who we are from the start. Let's do it that way."

It sounded daunting to Hayley, to think of herself – of them, the couple – as a brand now. But that was the idea. This concept wasn't particularly unique, but it had meaning for them both.

"And look, there's still plenty of time for us to go shopping and say our last goodbyes to Paris," Veronica told her as they strolled, arm in arm, out of the salon. "Mm, just smell that lovely summer air."

"It's going to be hotter back home. Can you imagine?"

Even though they had only been in Paris for a month and a half, Hayley could not imagine what it would be like back home. Everything about her life seemed to center on Veronica. This woman was her everything. They had done more in months than Hayley expected to try in a lifetime. Each night, she loved that she fell asleep with Veronica's arms around her. In the morning, she loved opening her eyes to see that face only inches from hers.

What would her family say when they saw her in a few days? They were flying to Omaha the next morning, getting settled into their new digs, and then…

The family visit was inevitable.

Hayley didn't worry about their judgment about her relationship, so much as their questions about her path in life. They would wonder why she gave up her dream – a perfectly normal dream that would have done them proud and, she assured them for so many years, made her happy. What were they going to say when she told them what she'd decided to do instead?

"Hey." Veronica gave her arm a little jiggle. "You're a million miles away and we haven't even set foot on the airplane yet."

"I know. It's just that I'm still trying to figure out what my parents are going to say when we get there."

"Yeah, you're all about knowing what's going to happen, instead of trusting that the unknown isn't necessarily bad. But let me lay it out for you." Veronica pulled Hayley closer so they could link elbows. "Your parents are going to love me because everyone loves me.

Then you're going to wow them with your new plan for your life, and they're going to decide college tuition was money well spent."

"I don't know if you're trying to be funny or what." Hayley grimaced. Veronica knew full-well her parents hadn't paid a dime toward college for her because Hayley didn't want them too.

"Or what," Veronica clarified.

As they rounded a corner, Hayley tried to think of how to phrase her next question. "Veronica?"

"Yes?"

"How are you forty-years-old and so..."

"Vibrant? Amazing? Fun?"

Hayley rolled her eyes. "I was thinking immature."

"Ah, I hate that perception of age as meaning something." Veronica reached up to scrub her hands over her face. "Look, Hayley, age literally is just a number. Of course, I'd like to think that now I'm in my forties, I know how to not just have a good time, but how to be responsible while doing it. Spontaneity and a sense of humor aren't traits of immaturity. They're me being true to myself. I face up to my responsibilities, whatever they are. My humor is off-beat, sure, but sometimes we need that to keep from going crazy in this world."

Even though they were standing on the sidewalk, Veronica turned to her and pressed a kiss to her lips. The affectionate gesture took her breath away and she gave into it, leaning against Veronica and letting her eyes close.

When they separated, they kept their foreheads pressed together, noses touching. "I love you just as you are," Hayley said, "quirks and all."

"Good, because I feel the same way about you." Veronica twirled a strand of Hayley's hair around her finger and smiled. "But this modern cut looks good on you. I'm sure anything would look good on you."

Hayley finally smiled and nodded. "Then let's go buy some things that look good on us both. We need to be ready for the future."

By the time they were done, Hayley was surprised they had controlled themselves so well. Then again, they did have packing limitations to consider. They stopped at a café for a late lunch – one last opportunity to eat at one of the tables outdoors in the sunlight and watch the passersby.

It was like a completely different world, Hayley mused as she looked at the people around them. "I love this country," she said, resting her chin on her hand while holding her coffee cup with the other. "It's even better than what I imagined from books and movies. Can we come back sometime soon?"

"I like that idea," Veronica said. "Tell you what – we get the shop established and succeeding, then we'll celebrate its one-year anniversary with a return to Paris. How does that sound?"

"It sounds fantastic." Hayley looked up at the skyline, which included the Eiffel Tower, and shook her head. "This has been like a dream. I thought I'd get here someday but as a journalist. Not as someone's girlfriend, you know?"

"I know. This is the first time I've ever brought someone I love to Paris." Veronica let out a giggle and ducked her head. "I mean, my mother lives here, but that's not the kind of love I mean. I mean someone I chose – you. This has been as special for me as it has been for you and it's only going to keep getting better."

They joined hands across the table and Hayley looked down at where they touched each other. With Veronica at her side, she felt like she had been broken down, remade, and then fortified. She felt strong and certain of herself in a whole new way. They had a plan now, a shared dream, and she couldn't wait to see how it turned out.

Chapter 20

GETTING SETTLED IN OMAHA wasn't the hard part. They were both excited to be back in the United States and sign the papers on both their new home and shop. It would take a week for the movers to gather their belongings from D.C. and bring them halfway across the country, which was just enough time for Hayley to bring Veronica to meet her family.

"What's it like to drive this thing?" Veronica asked as the hills of eastern Nebraska diminished and flat land stretched along either side of the road.

Hayley shrugged. They had purchased a hybrid vehicle on their second day and she liked the way it ran. "It's like any other car," she said. "Except it's so quiet, you'd think it's not running when it's in park. Do you want to try?"

Veronica shifted in her seat and shrugged. "I need some practice before I try driving."

"Practice?" Hayley slid a glance at her girlfriend and then looked back at the road. "As in you haven't driven in a while?"

"That's it. I have my license, of course, but I've had drivers throughout my entire life. I can't remember the last time I had to drive on my own. If you don't mind, I'd like to try after the next rest area. I mean, if we have to stop again between here and there."

They'd already been on the road for two hours and stopped a half-hour prior. "We're only an hour away, but we can get some practice on the way back if you want."

"What's the name of this town again?"

"Scotia. It's just a little town, but I have to admit I like it." In fact, Hayley was getting even more excited as she turned onto the familiar roads that led to the family home. It had been her grandparents' and then her parents' home. She loved that she came from a long tradition of farmers. Unfortunately, her parents' business hadn't been so great over the past couple of decades.

It was a problem of growth, Hayley realized. They couldn't keep up with larger, better-equipped farms, so most of their income came from local farmer's markets instead of something larger or steadier. She hoped Amber's enthusiasm for the changes she had implemented that spring was still sustained now.

The farm was on the outskirts of Scotia and as Hayley rounded the curve, she saw the peak of the roof just beyond the trees. She expected the crunch of gravel beneath her tires, but the driveway looked freshly paved.

"That's new," she murmured as she maneuvered along its gentle curves.

"What's new?" Veronica asked.

"The driveway. It used to be gravel. I don't know how Mom and Dad got the funds to pay for that, but it's quite a... Oh!" She nearly stomped on the brakes in her surprise. "The house."

The weathered siding with hail damage was gone. Instead, there was fresh new white siding wrapping around the house. The roof looked new too and Hayley blinked several times as she put the car in park.

"It didn't look like that when I was here last Christmas," she told Veronica, still staring at the house. "I guess they did some work over the spring, though I can't imagine how they managed to afford it unless Aunt Regina's estate was generous enough to cover it."

"Aunt Regina?"

Hayley turned off the ignition and sat back in the

seat. "Yeah. She passed away right after Christmas and left everything to my mother. Amber told me it was enough to make some changes on the farm, but I didn't expect anything like this."

"Well, we can sit here staring or we can walk in there and find out."

"Yeah." Hayley let out a breath and nodded. "Yeah," she repeated. After another heartbeat, she unbuckled her seatbelt and opened the car door. She was glad she kept in touch with her family through emails and a couple of international phone calls. Otherwise, it would be a pretty awkward visit.

But they already knew she was bringing a girlfriend home – she'd been very specific about that – and that they were going into business together. Other than that, Hayley hadn't gone into details. Not even with her sister. She told Amber this was the kind of conversation she wanted to have face-to-face, not in an email.

"Hay!" Naturally it was Amber who greeted her first, flinging open the front door, yelling her nickname, and then running down the driveway followed by three big dogs.

"Amberston!" Hayley managed to keep her footing as her little sister threw herself into her embrace. The dogs were well-trained enough not to jump all over them, but they circled the girls, sniffing at Hayley's legs.

"I hope you brought me something from Paris," Amber said, stepping back and swiping her bangs out of her eyes. "Even a 'My sister went to Paris and all I got was this stupid t-shirt' shirt."

"I might have gotten you something like that." Hayley turned to Veronica and gestured between them. "Amber, you remember Veronica, right?"

"Of course I do." Amber stepped forward, glanced at Veronica's extended hand, and then hugged her. "Damn, it's good to have Hayley finally bring someone home. Especially someone as awesome as Veronica Stone. You are my favorite model of all time."

Hayley grinned as she ruffled the dogs' fur and stroked their soft ears, while her sister hugged Veronica. It was quite a sight to see and it reminded her just how lucky she was to have a loving family.

"Honestly, I'm not surprised the online news thing didn't work out for you," Amber said as she stepped away from Veronica. "And I'm glad, too. Glad this woman helped knock some sense into you."

"Ha." Veronica placed her hands on her hips and shook her head. "Trust me, it was all Hayley. She decided she couldn't compromise her integrity and ethics all in the name of a job she didn't actually want. I take no credit. This woman did all of this on her own."

Rising to her feet, Hayley tried to appear nonchalant, but she couldn't help but lower her gaze. She wasn't accustomed to receiving so many compliments.

"Holy crap, do you see that?" Amber crowed.

"I see that," Veronica said.

"What?" Hayley asked, lifting her head. "What is it?"

"You're blushing, big sis. I've never seen you do that in my entire life. I didn't even think you were capable of it. Always so down-to-earth and logical. Never emotional."

"Jeez." Hayley turned to glance around the yard and ran her hand through her hair.

"Also, nice haircut," Amber said, circling her almost the way the dogs had. "Seriously – it's cute. Modern. I never expected it."

Veronica's low laugh told Hayley just how amused her girlfriend was by all of this. Suppressing a grumble, Hayley looked at her sister again and smirked at her. "Fine, so I've changed. It's not that big a deal."

Amber lifted her hand and held her thumb and index finger an inch apart. "You haven't changed too much. Just enough," she said. "Just enough to let me know you've gone on a journey. I love it and I'm glad you're moving back to Nebraska. It's a heck of a lot closer than Washington D.C. But let's get inside. Mom and Dad want to see you both, and you said you wouldn't tell us anything about your plans until we were all face to face."

They followed Amber into the house and Hayley noticed the inside looked as fresh and new as the outside. "Okay, what happened here?" she asked her sister.

"Just wait and you'll find out. Mom, Dad!" Amber called, skipping ahead. "They're here!"

Hayley expected to be engulfed in her father's bear hug and then to stoop over to give her mother a more delicate embrace. But she hadn't expected her father to give that same bear hug to Veronica, complete with a hearty thump on the back.

When they were finally seated around the living room, her father said, "So now we get the visit. It's about time." His manner was only slightly gruff. Richard Becker was almost always an affable guy – the loud, loving heart of the family.

"I'm sorry it took so long," Hayley apologized as she sat on the loveseat next to Veronica, her hands clasped over her knees.

"Please." Richard waved the apology off. "You're an adult. We can't expect you to report into us all the time. You have complete independence now. Then again…" He turned his attention to Veronica. "My Hayley has been completely independent since she was a teenager. She kind of had to be, but she let us know she was ready."

"I'm not surprised, Mr. Becker," Veronica said with one of her softer smiles. "Hayley doesn't like to rely on anyone but herself."

"Exactly, so you have no idea how happy we are that she found someone she trusts and loves enough outside of the family to bring into her life like this." Richard pushed himself out of his chair and said, "Speaking of which, we have something special for you, Veronica."

Hayley looked at her girlfriend and shrugged wordlessly. What could her father possibly have for Veronica? He'd never met her, didn't even really know her other than the fact that she was his oldest daughter's girlfriend.

But when he came back, Hayley saw it and it took her breath away.

"Wow," Veronica said, accepting the magazine and holding it almost reverently. "How did you find this?"

"My sister Regina," Hayley's mother spoke up. "She was an avid reader of *Vogue* and I inherited all of her issues when she passed away earlier this year. That, among other things, anyway. Well, when Amber met you at Hayley's graduation, she recognized your cover and we thought you might want it."

Hayley leaned over to look at it. There was Veronica, perhaps seventeen-years-old, and pouting at the camera for one of the spring issues of *Vogue*. "That's fantastic," Hayley whispered. "I've never seen your early work – just the more recent stuff."

"Well, we want you to keep it," Richard said, settling in his chair again. "If you want it, of course."

Somehow the chatter flowed more and more amiably, everyone getting to know each other. But it seemed to Hayley they got along like old friends with very little effort. She hadn't expected it to be this easy. Why had she worried all this time about her family questioning her choices after graduation?

In another hour, her mother, sister, and Veronica were in the kitchen, working on dinner together, and Hayley was strolling through the backyard with her father.

"So a coffee shop, eh?" he said.

"That's right. What do you think?" Hayley was back to wondering, worrying, and holding her breath.

"I think…" Richard hesitated and picked up a smooth white stone. The dogs had run ahead and then stopped to sniff around the edge of the duck pond. Richard stopped and skimmed the stone along the water's surface. "I think you've always known your own mind, Hayley. I've never been able to tell you what to do or how to do it, and you've done just fine without me.

But I have one piece of advice and I hope you'll listen to it."

Hayley nodded and waited for her father to share his advice. Considering he wasn't usually one for telling people what to do or how to do it, this surprised her.

"Don't be all work and no play," he said. "I know when you were younger you thought you were a burden to us, that you were in the way of us working and getting things done. But you never were. You were always loved. We just saw that you were capable of handling things on your own, so we let you run with it. We figured you'd be more prepared for life if we respected your independence, instead of getting in your way."

"Wow, Dad, I didn't realize you felt that way."

Richard gave a slight shrug and nodded toward the fields beyond the yard. "You seemed happy to take the reins, so I'm not surprised you decided to let go of them for a change. How did that feel?"

With a deep breath, Hayley followed his gaze to the cornfields and smiled. "It felt glorious," she finally said. "A little scary at first, though. I thought people would think I was a flake for quitting my new job and trotting off to another country."

"You? A flake?" Richard guffawed and shook his head. "Honey, what you are is overworked and underpaid. It's about time you let go and blew around like a rowboat on the ocean, instead of always holding the rudder. Your arms get tired, don't you know?"

Hayley laughed too and leaned against her father. "So I take it you approve of everything I've done since graduation?"

"Veronica, the coffee shop, the whole nine yards. And even if I didn't, you wouldn't let that stop you. You're just not that kind of girl." Richard put his arm around her shoulders and gave them a squeeze. "So what do you think of the home improvements?"

"They're gorgeous. I'm glad things have turned around," Hayley said.

"Me too. We miss your aunt, but since she had no heirs, your mother inherited her entire estate. We've put it to good use and Regina would have approved."

Hayley felt tears prick momentarily at her eyes at the thought of her aunt and her generosity in leaving everything to her mother. "Is Mom doing okay?"

"She's doing much better. Amber has taken over most of her responsibilities and she hired Ron and Benito. They've been a huge help. They even got Amber in on their harebrained scheme to make wine. Grapes, Hayley, we're growing grapes here. Can you imagine? Of course, it's a load off your mother's mind to have all of Aunt Regina's money going into what we need. I know you don't need anything from us, but you know you can ask if you do, right?"

"Yes, Dad, I know I can ask." Hayley sighed as she looked out over the landscape and let go of her worries. Even though she knew the only opinion that mattered was her own, it felt good to have her family validate her choices. That and to accept her girlfriend.

What a long way she'd come since being a wide-eyed college freshman, ready to take on the world.

Now she was embarking on a completely unexpected venture all because she chose love, a venture that felt perfectly right.

Chapter 21

"AND THEN I TOLD him he needed to move it a smidge to the right or risk my wrath." Veronica fluffed her hair and stretched. Normally, she would have done something like that in preparation to go out, but she was completely naked and standing in front of the shower.

Hayley finished tossing her clothes into the hamper and shook her head. "Please. You wouldn't harm a hair on the guy's head unless he really deserved it."

"Still, the sign has to be perfect." Veronica turned on the shower and flicked her fingers in the water. Water temperature was one of the few things they couldn't agree on. Hayley liked it lukewarm and Veronica liked it burning hot. They had found a comfortable middle ground for showering together, which made Hayley happy.

She had to admit, saving water appealed to her, but not as much as the intimacy of the shared evening routine.

"What is it?" Veronica had turned around to watch her.

"Nothing. Is the water warm yet?"

"It is and it's not nothing. It's something." Veronica straightened and drew back the shower curtain. "I can tell it's something because you're blushing again. Not that I'm complaining – it's adorable – but it means you're thinking super sweet or super naughty thoughts. I hope it's the second one."

"It's you." Taking a step forward, Hayley pressed her lips to Veronica's in a gentle kiss. "It's us. I love that we do this together every night, after spending the day handling different things at work. We get to come back around to each other, have dinner, take a shower, and then just be together."

Veronica pulled her into an embrace and Hayley couldn't help but giggle. "What is it?" Veronica asked softly.

"We're naked," Hayley muttered, sniffing at the blonde hair tickling her nose. "We're having a big, naked hug."

After another moment, they stepped into the shower and Veronica drew her under the hot spray of water. Even though Hayley didn't like it so hot, she closed her eyes and let the warmth envelop her.

It was nearly autumn now, so hot water wasn't such a bad thing.

And it was nearly time for the coffee shop's grand opening, too.

The timing was perfect, Hayley thought, for their ribbon-cutting. Could it get any better?

"Sweetie, are you happy?" Veronica's question came from out of the blue and Hayley blinked as she processed it.

"Yes, very happy. Why?"

"Well, I can't always tell with you. I just wanted to make sure. You've gone through a lot of changes in the past six months. I mean, you went from single to living with me, from working as a journalist back to being a barista. Are you sure it's what you want?"

Hayley was sure she wanted all of it, but she knew words weren't always the way to respond. So she stepped back under the spray and wrapped her arms around Veronica. She had more than words to express her feelings, just how right all of this was for her. With soapy skin against soapy skin, kisses and touches,

Hayley made sure Veronica knew exactly how she felt about her and where they were now.

They stayed warm through the night, tangled in each other until the morning light spilled into the bedroom.

"It's time," Veronica whispered.

"Mm…" As much as Hayley wanted to get up and get to work, she held onto Veronica's arm and pulled her back into bed. "Let's wait just one more minute."

"You never ask for one more minute." Veronica lay back down facing her.

Hayley finally blinked her eyes completely open and looked at the face looking back at her. "Hey," she finally said, her voice still husky with sleep.

"Hey." Veronica let out a low giggle. "Hey, Hay."

"Today's the day."

"It is." Veronica's lips curved in a soft small. "How do you feel, going back to your barista roots?"

Burrowing a little deeper under the covers, Hayley inhaled the scent on them. It was heady and floral – Veronica's shampoo, a smell she had come to appreciate. "I feel amazing about it," she said. "There's no pressure in serving coffee, you know? I mean, there is, but not like there was in making sure I wrote the right words, the ones people wanted to read."

"Yeah, but we're doing more than just serving coffee," Veronica murmured, scooting closer to her.

"Right. I mean, we do own the place." Hayley rolled over and clapped her hand against her forehead. "Oh, wow. We. Own. The. Place."

"Uh-huh, and then there's the fact that every cup of coffee is for a good cause."

Hayley grinned and looked back at Veronica. "Changing the world one cup at a time?"

"Right now I'd settle for changing you from a sleepy person into a wide-awake one, and I have a feeling one cup is what it will take. I'll start the coffee." Veronica got out of bed, then turned and pointed over her shoulder. "And I'm ordering a new coffeemaker, whether you want one or not. It's time we get one we can set to turn on before we wake up, not this one-cup thing we have to fight over. How long have I been telling you to get rid of it?"

"There have been other priorities," Hayley pointed out. Like investing her life savings into the coffee shop.

She refused to let Veronica take it on one hundred percent. Fifty-fifty was her motto. For the most part.

She certainly didn't keep score. The give and take was mutual. At first, Hayley had found settling into a relationship complicated, even frightening, but it truly had become everything she thought it could be.

The scent of coffee drifting from the kitchen finally galvanized her into motion. Soon she strolled into the kitchen wearing jeans and a white tank top. "Now who's ready for the day?" she asked, gesturing to herself.

"It looks like you are." Veronica wrapped her arm around Hayley's waist, setting her heart aflutter all over again as she offered her the cup of coffee. "For you, my lady."

"This is just what I need to cut a ribbon." Hayley sauntered around the loft apartment as she sipped the coffee. She loved the buildings in the Old Market. The fact that they had been able to buy a building with a shop on the bottom floor and an apartment on the second floor was wonderful. Instead of plain drywall from floor to ceiling, it had exposed brick and large windows that let in the light. Filling it with their stuff had been fun.

But putting together the coffee shop? Fabulous. And today was opening day.

Hayley couldn't wait to get everything up and running. So she downed the coffee and brought the cup back in the kitchen. "Okay, I'm ready to go."

"Are you sure?" Veronica looked stunning dressed down in her blue jeans and a cocoa brown t-shirt. She was bent over the stove, checking on a sheet of cinnamon rolls in the oven.

"Yeah, I'm sure. Let's eat and then get our butts in gear."

As soon as they were done with breakfast, they went downstairs to open the coffee shop and get everything started. They had missed the morning rush, but they hoped opening during the lunch hour would work in their favor.

Considering all their publicity over the past couple of months, they knew the word was out and people were interested. As the coffee started percolating and the ovens started cooking the pastries, there was a small crowd gathering outside.

"Oh wow, they're actually here." Veronica rubbed

her hands together and then shook them out. "I can't believe I'm a little nervous."

"It's your first time doing something that doesn't involve a magazine or behind-the-scenes do-gooding," Hayley said as she checked the tie on Veronica's apron and then her own. "There's giving an interview or a presentation, and then there's serving people coffee. Don't worry. Just follow my lead."

Together they approached the double doors, then opened them to the crowd. As soon as the doors were latched open, gold and white confetti sprinkled down as customers walked in.

"Welcome to The Love Brew," Veronica said, lifting her arm like a game show hostess.

Hayley giggled and bowed her head. It was perfect – completely perfect. She hurried behind the cash register to start taking orders.

Despite her nervousness, Veronica had no problem serving coffee and taking out the pastries as soon as they were ready. She talked the patrons up, kept the edibles freshly stocked, and helped Hayley when she needed an extra hand making drinks.

"Wow, this has been really fun," Veronica said at the end of the day as they sat on the plush café chairs, their feet elevated. "I can't believe it was a successful first day."

"Right? We caught the lunch and late afternoon crowds. I guess what I can't believe is that we have to be up at five in the morning to do this even earlier." Hayley sighed and leaned her head back. "That means we better get to bed early."

"I'm fine with that. Early nights with you just to get up at the crack of dawn with you? Heck yeah." After tallying the receipts for the day, Veronica grinned. "Look at how much we made."

Hayley sat upright and looked. "Is that right?"

"Yup and can you believe we're donating ten percent of that to PFLAG?"

"Fantastic." Hayley rested her chin on her hand and looked down at the receipt. "It's a powerful feeling, knowing a person can buy something as simple as a cup of coffee and donate to a good cause."

They exchanged smiles.

"That's a heck of a lot of Benjamins," Veronica

reaffirmed.

"More than I've ever seen in even one paycheck," Hayley said.

Her girlfriend's eyes went wide. "We're going to need to hire help if business keeps up this way."

"And we're going to need to consider added seating in the back room we haven't even finished yet." Hayley rose from the chair and gestured for Veronica to follow her lead. "One thing at a time, though. This was just day one."

It seemed strange that her life had come full circle like this, Hayley thought as they turned out the lights and walked upstairs. Who aspired to serve coffee? Certainly not her. But she had never thought about getting into journalism for fame or fortune.

Now she had it all – her own business doing something that felt right while giving back to a cause, and then there was Veronica. She managed to look like a model, even in her apron, with her hair pinned behind her head, carrying a serving tray…

Veronica.

Hayley turned and looked at her. It was hard to

believe their hot, anonymous sex had turned into this.

After dinner and their nighttime routine, they tumbled into bed together. Hayley snuggled up to her and sighed, her breath fanning over Veronica's skin.

"What's going on, my lady love?" Veronica sounded tired but playful.

"I was just thinking about how we met." Wistfulness crept into Hayley's voice. She couldn't help it. Something about the past six months was emblazoned in her mind as the most meaningful time of her life.

Veronica rolled over and smiled. "You're stuck in nostalgia-land, sweetie. You've been like this all day."

"I just can't help it. It's been a pretty wild ride for the past five months."

"Yeah." Veronica took Hayley's hand in hers. The warmth of their joined hands brought tears to Hayley's eyes and she blinked rapidly.

The tears, however, didn't go anywhere. They trickled down her cheeks and she reached up to dash them away with her fingertips. "Seriously, this is not what I expected at all and I'm so glad you're in my life, Veronica. So glad."

Hayley took a deep, shuddering breath, aware that the tears weren't stopping.

"My entire life was planned out and then I met you. Everything turned upside down and I'm so grateful." Her voice shook and she felt foolish for showing so much emotion, but there was no preventing it. "So grateful."

"Oh, Hayley." Veronica drew her into her arms and Hayley was surrounded by her scent again, just as she had been that morning. "I'm so grateful to you, too. I was not a happy person. You helped me discover what it means to be happy and to love someone. Now I'm doing something that matters with someone who matters. You changed, but I changed too, so thank you for that."

And then Veronica brought Hayley back to where it all began...

Titles by the Author

Something About You

Must Love Chickens

Meant to Be

Game of Hearts

All For Love

A Vote for Love

Series

A Charmed Life: The Ashland Witches, Book 1

A Garden Dream: The Ashland Witches, Book 2

(coming summer 2017)

About the Author

Jea Hawkins writes sweet and spicy contemporary lesbian romance. If love conquers all, then she'd like to think her heroines can rule the world one day. An east coast transplant to the Midwest, she loves to write about complicated women and settings that feel like home.

Personal addictions include autumn, cozy sweaters, hot chocolate, and the Sims 3. She's both an avid reader and gamer, and hopes readers don't mind a few geeky references here and there in her work.

You can keep up with her latest releases by signing up for her mailing list at http://eepurl.com/cVU-pz or by visiting her online at jeahawkins.com.

Printed in Great Britain
by Amazon

32634874R00165